STORIES OF
THE CHEROKEE HILLS

"JUDAS! YOU OLD COON!" — "MARS BEN!" (Page 72)

STORIES OF
THE CHEROKEE HILLS

BY

MAURICE THOMPSON

Short Story Index Reprint Series

BOOKS FOR LIBRARIES PRESS
FREEPORT, NEW YORK

First Published 1898
Reprinted 1970

STANDARD BOOK NUMBER:
8369-3415-6

LIBRARY OF CONGRESS CATALOG CARD NUMBER:
77-113686

PRINTED IN THE UNITED STATES OF AMERICA

CONTENTS

	Page
Color-Line Jocundities	1
Ben and Judas	34
Hodson's Hide-Out	78
Rudgis and Grim	115
A Race Romance	139
A Dusky Genius	169
The Balance of Power	216

LIST OF ILLUSTRATIONS

PAGE

"Judas! you old coon!" — "Mars Ben!"
(Page 72) . . . . . *Frontispiece*

Side by side on the sandy bank of the
stream 48

"W-w-w'at Dave is yer tarkin' 'bout?" . 102

Grim 116

He filled his pipe, and lighted it . . 134

"Call me Mr. Marting" 160

He watched this strange procession . . 166

Judge Dillard 178

STORIES OF THE CHEROKEE HILLS

COLOR–LINE JOCUNDITIES

HISTORY is the record of closed periods, the presentation of what mankind has lost and gained in the course of progress. When I was a boy Bud Peevy said to me: "Ef ye 'r' a-hankerin' ter know what ye don't want ter know, jes' ax a ole man what he thinks o' a young un." Bud was, himself, neither young nor old. "I kin look both ways," he often remarked, "an' see back inter the what wus an' for'rd inter the goin' ter be. They's both poorty much erlike. What wus did n't sat'sfy nobody, an' what's er goin' ter be 'll never make no livin' soul happy. We loses an' we finds; but we never finds ag'in what we loses, an' we never has a dern thing wo'th er huntin' fer when we 've lost it." I am neither accepting nor rejecting Bud Peevy's philosophy; what I feel is that history must be valuable in proportion to the accuracy of its details, and that its most precious details are those incidents of human life that flicker along the vanishing line by which the close of every period of civilization is momentarily marked.

Early in my childhood our family went to live on a lonely estate amid the mountains of Cherokee Georgia. The farmstead was circled around by foothills, above which in all directions blue peaks kissed the rim of a heaven that looked like the half of a pale blue bird-egg shell turned hollow side down. All of our neighbors and friends were mountaineers, and I grew up a mountaineer boy. I spoke the mountain lingo, wore the mountain garb, conformed to all the customs and manners of the mountain folk for many years, and, indeed, was scarcely less than to the manner born.

With a flint-lock, " whole-stock " rifle I
shot in competition at the matches for beef
and turkey; I danced at many a cabin ball
where the fiddler played " Natchez under
the Hill," " Black-Eyed Susan," " Cotton-
Eyed Joe," and "Flat Woods," and where
the loose board floor rattled merrily under
our jigging feet.   I went to singing-school
and to class-meeting, to weddings and to
funerals, to still-house meets ; I went coon-
hunting by torchlight, chestnut-hunting on
the mountain tops, 'possum-hunting in the
bottom lands, and was always present at
the particular justice court ground where
a fight was expected.   Moreover I chewed
" mounting-twist " tobacco and smoked the
same, until I became aware of better habits and reformed.

Certainly in those wild, free days I did
not dream of "local color" or of literary
materials.   It was a mountaineer who
taught me the use of the longbow; but I
never expected to use it in history, or in

fiction, not more than I looked forward to the influence that Theocritus — whose Idylls were even then being drilled into me by a private tutor — might have upon my unthought-of poetry. Yet it must be seen that my life was flushing itself, flooding me, with the elements that have perforce entered into the sketches here offered to the historian of American civilization.

When the great war came on I went into it, hot-headed, unthinking, a mere boy, bubbling over with enthusiasm for the South and its cause. Fortune so directed that I was to be a mountaineer even in military life, and for many months I served as a scout in the rugged, billowy region of North Georgia, North Alabama, and East Tennessee. At the close of the war I went back to our home in the hills, resuming for a while the old life; as Bud Peevy would say: "A livin' 'twixt starvation an' the 'tater patch," with a book in one hand and a hoe in the other, while a vague yet irresistible impulse compelled me to seek literary expression. Then men and women began to be objects of absorbing curiosity. I studied them with hungry persistence, but found myself attempting to describe and portray only the men and women that I had read about; and it was not until after I had gone into Indiana and made my home there that I became aware of the Southern mountaineer as a persistent and insistent supplicant for portraiture at my hands.

Now, albeit the war was ended, politics had taken on the bitterness engendered by the reconstruction troubles, and when these sketches on the "color-line," written early in the seventies, were offered to editors they were promptly rejected, on the ground that "fiction in any way connected with the recent war in the South and its results" could not fail to "engender ill feeling and do injury to both writer and publisher." So my stories of slavery, war, emancipation, and reconstruction in the Southern mountain region were cast aside and lay in the manuscript for years, until at last, after I had printed other stories, and after the impression of the great war had somewhat softened, I offered one of them, entirely rewritten and very much changed, to the "Century Magazine" under the title, "Hodson's Hide-Out," and it was promptly accepted and printed. The other stories in this volume followed, all, except "The Balance of Power," appearing at intervals in the "Century;" the last named story was printed in "Harper's Magazine," and to the editors of these great publications I am indebted for the privilege of offering this book to the world.

The reader will not need to be told that these bits of fiction were written with the purpose to fix in imperishable, even if crude, form the curious effects wrought by negro slavery upon the lives of the illiterate, stubborn, and absolutely independent dwellers among the arid and almost inaccessible mountains of the South. I knew my people, and little as I could trust my art, I could not doubt the accuracy or the value of that knowledge, no matter how imperfectly it might be set in literature.

There is no caricature in these stories; the mist of fiction and the sheen of imagination have not distorted the main facts as I saw them in their day. Slavery in the mountains was very little like slavery in the low country, and the reader need not hesitate to accept as true, albeit clothed upon with romance, the singular features most prominent in these excerpts from a life not to be measured by the standard of any other. The story of " Ben and Judas " represents not Middle Georgia proper, but rather the hill country now called " Piedmont Georgia," where it borders the real mountain region. I give it first place because it was first written (although " Hodson's Hide-Out " preceded it in publication, as I have said), and because it sounds the key-note of my purpose.

The mountaineers proper rarely owned slaves; only here and there one had been willing or able to buy a black. Of course there were many prosperous farmers in the Cherokee country, many wealthy slave-owners; but they were not mountaineers. Indeed, nearly all of the rich "river-bottom" lands and most of the fertile valley plantations were the property of aristocratic low-country planters, who had come into the hills after the "land-lottery" days. The mountaineers clung to the "pockets" and coves, preferring the broken country far from railroads and towns. One or two negroes could be found on some of the forlorn little farms where accident or unusual thrift had favored a man like Rudgis, and in a few cases a master like Dillard was a fair example of a hybrid, neither a mountaineer nor a low-countryman.

It struck me that the attitude of the

mountaineer toward slavery and emancipation would give just the touch of serio-comic oddity needed to set the "vanishing line" of the old régime most tellingly before the public. The impression haunted me so that I returned to the mountain country and studied over again the details of life there, collecting from every available source the materials used in my sketches. When these were refused by the editors upon both business and political grounds, I felt to a degree the justice of the criticism, considering the state of public sentiment at both the North and the South just then. And even when the stories did appear in the magazines, they were strenuously objected to by some Southern extremists as being favorable to Northern prejudices, while, on the other hand, many Northern readers, especially in New England, castigated me severely for my sympathy with the slaveholder and the "Lost Cause"! Between the two armies of objectors I felt timid about printing the stories in book form, and so they have lain until now.

I would not have it understood that I magnify the importance of these stories, as stories. I am keenly aware of their many imperfections. They are offered as sidelights to history. Dunk Roe of Pinelog assured me in a talk, written down in 1896, — a late date in the breaking-up period, — that " ef er feller air inter a noshen thet er nigger air es good es er white man, thet air feller needs hell three times er day." But Dunk Roe was, and probably still is, a politician to be classed morally with those Northerners who deem it their duty to cram the negro forcibly into the cars, the theatres, the schools, and the churches built, owned, and operated by white Southerners for the use of white Southerners.

The color-line is not a line of disgrace to black or white. There would be no trouble on it, if it were respected by man as thoroughly as God respected it in creating the two races. Dunk Roe said: "God A'mighty air 'sponsible fer the black on er nigger an' fer the white on er white man. Hit ain't no disgrace fer er nigger ter be er nigger, ner fer er white man ter be er white man. Hit air w'en er nigger tries ter be white, an' er white man wrassles ter be er nigger, 'at the disgrace comes in." The "Race Romance" exhibits a white man who felt called upon to do missionary work with the purpose of reversing the order of things on the color-line. Peevy says that "what thet air nigger finally an' everlastin'ly done ter thet dern white man do p'intedly show jes' what 'd happing ter all the white folks o' this kentry ef them dad ding nigger-lovers hed ther way."

In writing these sketches it was my aim to occupy an impartial point of view. I told my old friend Brimson, some time before his experiment wrecked him, that I had no argument to offer for or against

the theory that he so enthusiastically main-
tained; but Dunk Roe spoke freely to
him, in nearly these words: —

" Brimson, hit air er fac' 'at ye hain't got
half sense; but er dern fool orter know 'at
ye cayn't edicate er nigger in fifteen
minutes so 'at he kin be like er white man.
Hit hev tuck erbout er million years to
edicate the white man an' mek 'im reason-
able decent; an' how the dernation kin ye
'spect ter tek er eejit nigger an' mek a ekal
ter the white man of 'im?   An' 'spacially
wi' er triflin' ole sap-head, like ye air, fer
ter do it."

In the course of my latest inquiries I
talked with an intelligent old negro named
Tuck Baker, an original character, if there
ever was one.   Before and during the war
he belonged to 'Squire Baker on Pinelog.
I inquired about him before seeing him,
and was not surprised when, to one of my
direct questions, he made answer: —

" Ya-a-s, sah, boss, I done voted one

time at de 'lection, an' dat's 'nuff fo' Tuck. Ya-a-s, sah."

He wagged his grizzled woolly head and grinned with reminiscent opulence of expression, his face shining like a gargoyle polished with lampblack.

" Ya-a-s, sah, I done put in one vote, an' cotch it in de yea' good an' hard fo' it; ya-a-s, sah."

" How was that, Tuck?" I inquired with insinuating emphasis.

" How wus it? Yo' ax how wus it? Well, sah, boss, hit wus lak er bein' kicked wid er fo' yea' ole mule; dat's jes' 'zac'ly how it wus."

Tuck was a huge man; nor had his sixty-five years lessened the solidity of his ebon bulk of muscles. As he stood before me, grinning and gazing aslant reflectively, he gave me the fullest impression of half-savage humor strongly affected by a very noteworthy and wholly comical recollection.

"Ya-a-s, sah, boss, I chuck one vote in-ter de box; an' I wus er feelin' ez big es er skinned hoss on dat 'casion, kase dem whi' men wus all stan'in' roun' er lookin' at me while I say: 'Yar go my senterments;' an' jes' den I feel somep'n'."

He chuckled and shook his head with a certain indescribable expression of jocund-ity.

"Ya-a-s, sah, I feel somep'n' what jar dis yer ole haid same lak er bar'l er co'n been drap on it. I 'spec I went er whollopin' heel ober haid pooty nigh erbout seben-teen feet en struck de groun' on de back o' my haid. Ya-a-s, sah, I did fall outda-cious hard; en den I year er whi' man say: 'Dat 's my senterments, yo darn black whelp!' Ya-a-s, sah, dat 's jes' w'at he say, en he 's de one 'at hit me en mighty nigh bus' my haid."

He pressed his big black hand on his ear, as if he still felt the effect of the buffet.

"Ya-a-s, sah, I 's not b'en er doin' berry

much votin' sence dat day. Yah, yah, yahee!"

His laugh was atrociously, barbarously charged with delight in his reminiscence.

"Boss," he presently added, "is yo' 'quainted wid Mistah Bud Peeby?"

I nodded affirmatively.

"Well, sah, boss, 't wus him 'at knock de votin' notion clean out 'n me. Yah, yah, yahee-e-e!"

And between Brimson and Peevy lies an area which, doubtless, is the land of the golden mean. Tuck seemed satisfied, nay stimulated, as he thus sketched, with dramatic strokes distinctly African, his one experience at the polls; and I saw that he fully realized the beauty of the inevitable.

"Ya-a-s, sah, boss," he remarked in conclusion, giving his clouted trousers an upward jerk, "ya-a-s, sah, boss, I done retired f'om polertics, sho 's yo' bo'n! I done aterwards tole Mistah Bud Peeby 'at it seem lak his senterments is mo' stronger 'n mine.

Ya-a-s, sah, I done tole 'm dat. No, sah, boss, I 's not hongry ter vote no mo', yah, yah, yahee-e-e! Sho 's yo' bo'n I 's done fill plum' full an' er runnin' ober, — I done got er plenty; don' wush no mo'. I done tole Mistah Bud Peeby 'at he kin do my votin' fo' me; ya-a-s, sah."

Upon the whole, however, the change from master and slave to boss and freed-man has generated no deep troubles. Peevy and Tuck are excellent friends as they toe the color-line. They regard each other with humorous respect, comprehend-ing the situation far more clearly than do the good zealots who from afar off shout for equality. The black and white are ar-ranging the difficult details of their rela-tions by the law of Nature, a law which no legislative body can successfully modify or amend, which no earthly power can repeal. And what a picturesque civilization the two colors are forming!

The line fades more slowly in the moun-

tain region than it does in the most aristocratic part of the low country.   Education
is a sponge that wipes out prejudice, which
is the only real stumbling-block of Chris-
tian people black and white.   But education proceeds slowly when it has to climb
rocky steeps and stumble along inhospi-
table fells.   Besides, the mountaineers re-
sent every hint of change, every suggestion from outside their customs and habits,
every apparition of authority; and they
cannot understand how a man, sitting away
off yonder as a court of law, can have the
right to send another man, as a sheriff, to
meddle with their affairs.   Hodson had no
conception of the right of Confederate or
Federal officials to order him into war or
to bid him let go his slave.   So the distil-
ler of " mounting jew " whiskey at this moment has no sense of transgression on his
part, when he resists the revenue squad ;
but it seems certain to him that the government is an outlaw.

" Hit use ter be right fer every man 'at wanted to ter build 'im er still-house an' mek all the licker 'at he wushed to," said Lige Hackett, " an' I jes' cay n't see how hit's any wronger now 'an hit wus then. I 'd jes' shoot seving diffe'nt sorts o' liver an' lights outen any gov'ment jay-hawker 'at 'ud kem foolin' 'roun' my place er bizness, an' don't ye fergit it!"

Now, in the days when I was a mountaineer I rolled all of these elementary philosophic peculiarities under my tongue as morsels sweet as honey-wax from Arcadia. With every breath from the hills of Habersham, with every waft from Rabun, or Estell, or from the wild pockets of Dade, I drew in unlimited love of savage, absolute freedom. I got firmly footed upon the ground occupied by Peevy and Rudgis and Hodson. But I trod the color-line with a full appreciation also of those genial and faithful grotesques who ploughed and hoed and sang so blithely in the fields

of corn and cotton. Ah! the old days, —
call them quasi-feudal, call them a faded
and feeble reflection of mediæval romance,
give them what bitter name you will, — I
tell you that they were like old mellow wine,
and the smack of them can never quit the
tongue that tasted them. The dance in
the big house and the hoe-down in the
kitchen, it were hard to say which was the
merrier. The blacks worked; but never
before, since Eve ate and Adam gorged to
purchase a curse, did laborers seem to have
so good a time at their tasks. The whites
played from morning till night; yet all
play and no work did not sour the life they
lived.

The few negroes owned by mountaineers were coddled as precious pet animals
sometimes are. Even men like Peevy were
over-indulgent masters, strictly as they insisted upon every formality of the color-
line. The story of "Ben and Judas" indi-
cates one of the curious results of constant

and long personal familiarity between ex-
ceptional individuals of the two races where
the slackest state of thralldom and the
warmest sort of sympathy ruled conditions.
It is a sketch from life. In my childhood
I knew the men, and in my youth I heard
the story of the melon-patches and the
prayer over the delicious plunder. Indeed,
it was while on a pedestrian ramble in
" Piedmont Georgia," as the late Mr.
Grady, the gifted editor and orator, named
the lower hill country, that I (searching
for a few bits of local color needed in re-
vising " Ben and Judas ") fell upon high
fortune in making the acquaintance of
Mr. Hector Aaron Lifter, M. A.   He was
a clever yellow man, a graduate and post
graduate of an obscure Northern college,
and absorbed in self-conceit while osten-
sibly doing educational missionary work
among the blacks, whom he patronizingly
spoke of as " My people."

I had little to do with Lifter; but I am

infinitely indebted to him for a collection
of curious rhymes and crude ditties picked
up by him during two or three years of
commendable research and inquiry. Not
a few of the pieces in this collection have
been familiar to me from childhood ; but
there are many that appear to be of more
recent origin. Slaves were fond of grotesque music, which they often attempted
to imitate in metre and rhyme. Here are
a few examples of negro word-melody : —

> " Mule colt,
> Shuck collah,
> Blame mule
> Eat de collah,
> Cost ole massa
> Half er dollah."

" Hi, oh, Mariley come down de mountain,
     Ho, Mariley, ho-o-oh !
  Wid er sta' on 'is breas' an' er ring on 'is finger,
     Ho, Mariley, ho-o-oh !
  Hi, oh, Mariley look like er preacher,
     Ho, Mariley, ho-o-oh !
  But de Debbil tuck er chunk an' he burnt ole Mariley,
     Ho, Mariley, ho-o-oh ! "

Both of the foregoing examples are corn songs, that is, they were sung mostly at corn-huskings by night; but the following are field songs, probably improvised by ploughmen while trudging in the fragrant furrows across the bottom lands:—

" Grow, co'n, grow in de new groun' bottom,
        Grow, co'n, grow, yi ho-o-o !
Yo' heah me, co'n, den lissen w'at I tole yo',
        Grow, co'n, grow, ho-ee-hoee, ho ! "

" Dey 's er gal in de kitchen er bakin' de braid,
        Hilly, hally, hally ho, hi ho !
En dat gal's eye sorty twinkle in 'er haid,
        Hilly ho, hally ho, hi ho-o-o ! "

" Chicken, O chicken, is ye gwine ter roos' low?
        Roos' low, roos' low.
Fo' de big pot 's er bilin' ober de fire,
        Roos' low, roos' low,
En po' ole nig cay n't climb much higher,
        Roos' low, roos' low ! "

" Runt pig, runt pig, is yo' sho' yo' knows me ?
        Piggy, piggy, pig, pigoo !
Dey 's er nubbin er co'n in de basket fo' yo',
        Pigoo, pigoo, pigoo !

Runt pig, runt pig, fatten up faster,
  Piggy, piggy, pig, pigoo !
En w'en yo' 's gone ole mars' won't miss yo',
  Pigoo, pigoo, pigoo ! "

The pieces that are probably of early post-slavery date have an unwelcome touch of self-conscious sentiment in them. I need quote but one : —

" De ole time gone en I go too,
  De ole time gone erway.
Dey 's no mo' light in cabin doo',
  De ole time gone erway.
Wha' dem chill'en ? Wha' ole mudder ?
  De ole time gone erway.
Wha' ole marstah ? Wha' ole mist'ess ?
  De ole time gone erway."

But Paul Dunbar has shown that the native strain of poetry in the negro's nature can find much nobler utterance than these crude bits would have seemed to promise. I quote them merely to give the warrant I had for introducing certain negro songs of my own as coming from the lips of my black people. And it is well to note here that the negroes of the highlands were far more merry, genial, and musical than those of the lowlands. I once made a voyage down the Coosawattee River in a corn boat manned by negroes. Our way led us between incomparably rich plantations lying on either side of the stream ; but it was only now and then that we could see the fields, the banks being high and densely fringed with reeds. One of our crew had what the negroes called " quills ; " it was a rude syrinx, made (exactly to the ancient pattern) of graduated cane joints fastened together in a row, on which he played a barbaric tune while some of the others patted and danced.

In the night from the distant plantation quarters we often heard answering quills, whose strains softened by remoteness struck my sense with an indescribable dreamy pathos. One evening, while we lingered at an obscure ferry, a small party of slaves in charge of a good-natured over-

seer came down the little clay road to the
river, and spent awhile with us before
crossing.   One huge black fellow begged
the quills from our man, and blew so
sweetly on it that the tune rollics in my
memory to this day.   Another fellow, a
stripling with a face which was nearly all
mouth, sang a ditty of which I can give
but one stanza: —

"Side-meat en sweet 'taters eat mighty good,
    En my gal 's er gwine home in de mo'nin' ;
 Debbil say he 'bout ter die, don' yo' wush he would ?
    En my gal 's er gwine home in de mo'nin' ;
 Hip, hi, shuffle knee high,
    Fo' my gal 's er gwine home in de mo'nin'."

It was the sunny-minded, optimistic
negroes whose slavery days fell among the
mountains, and when one of them belonged
to a true highlander there was little danger that thralldom would be more or less
than an idyllic experience, well worth pre-
serving in art far more beautiful than
mine.   In one of my notebooks I find the

following nearly verbatim report of what Steve Iley told me about his negro: —

" He war nat'ly no ercount; but he cud play the banjer an' sing ter everlastin'. Folks use ter come clean f'om Ellijay " (a county seat fifteen miles distant) "to yer 'im pick an' sing 'is songs. I use to swa' ter myself 'at I 'd whirp 'im fo' not workin'; but he war so dad burn comic 'at I jes' cud n't keep f'om laughin' at 'im."

"And what became of him?" I inquired.

" W'at 'come er my nigger Tom? Oh, he's er livin' over the mounting yander. W'en the wa' freed 'im I druv 'im off'n my place 'cause he called me ' boss,' the dad burn ole vilyan."

I have never been able to hear of a single negro who has habitually used the word master since the war in personally address-ing his former owner, and the mountain-eer does not take kindly to being called boss.

That genial and gifted man, the author

of the "Uncle Remus" books, is of the opinion that Southern slaves knew but little about the banjo; the fiddle, he thinks, was their chief musical instrument. I make no controversy, and only know that in the mountains the white men fiddled and the blacks "picked de banjer." Many a time all night long have I obeyed the commands: "Swing yer pardners an' circle ter the lef'," "Sighshay," "First gentleman ter the lef', " "Balernce all," and the like, to the music of a home-made banjo played by a negro; but this was of course only when a fiddler could not be had.

I shall never forget an orchestra that we were honored with one night at the spacious cabin of Jere Borders, somewhere near the head waters of the Salliquoy. An octogenarian white fiddler, a fat negro banjoist, and a "straw drummer" were the musicians. The straw drummer's business was to beat time upon the fiddle strings during the playing. Late in the evening there was a misunderstanding, and most of us quit dancing and began a lively fight. Out went all the lights, save that from a flickering pine knot on the hearth, and there was hot work for five minutes in the dark. When it was all over, and we thought it time to resume the dance, Hank, the fat black banjoist, was missing, and after some search we found him up the chimney, where he was wedged in so fast that we had to pull him down by the legs; but so carefully had he guarded his beloved instrument that it was not even out of tune! It was that banjo of Hank's from which came the main suggestion of " A Dusky Genius." Hank himself took great delight in explaining to me how he wrought the rude yet beautiful lute, the head of which was covered with a translucent opossum-skin.

My own first lessons in banjo-picking were received from " old John," the coal-black property of Mr. Joseph Wilson,

whose plantation lay on the Coosawattee,
about seven miles northeast of Calhoun in
Gordon County, Georgia. Later a friend,
Mr. John O'Callaghan, of the same town,
left in my possession for some years an
excellent instrument made by a negro.
Indeed, I know that the slaves of the
mountain region were in many instances
very ingenious and skillful mechanics as
well as musicians. A curious lute was
made by one darkey thus: A gourd vine
was trained to grow along the ground, and
when a young gourd began to form, two
broad boards were driven parallel firmly
into the earth in such a position that as
the gourd grew it was forced to take a flat
form between them. When it had ripened
and hardened it was scraped and polished,
the handle sawed off, the insides neatly removed. Then a banjo-neck was fitted on,
sound-holes cut, a bridge and strings put
on, and lo! a banjo, the dry, hollow, thinly
flattened gourd serving as the body; and

a comical instrument it was, feeble, stupid sounding, but yet giving forth true notes.

The story entitled " The Balance of Power " brings another slight change on the color-line. Political currents swirled at random for some time in the South before the whites fairly got things to going their own way. In the low country the outcome has been through constitutional amendment, limiting the exercise of the elective franchise to citizens of lawful age who can read and satisfactorily explain to the proper board a section of the state organic law. Of course the board is composed of white men, and when I was in northern Mississippi, soon after the constitutional change began to operate in that State, I made some inquiries regarding the effect of it. I had followed the subsiding billows of the great Sand Mountain disturbance across Alabama, and was now beating around among the farewell hills. Aaron Harper explained the matter to me. Said he : —

" I never went ter no school, an' never hed no l'arnin', an' hit s'prised me mighty nigh inter fits w'en I suddently found out 'at I could read. Hit wus this way : I goes down ter town 'lection day ter vote, an' there 's ebout two hundred niggers trompin' eroun' on thet same business; but nary er dern one o' 'em could read thet constertootion. Well, sa', w'at ye s'pose I done w'en they stuck thet air docymint under my nose ? "

" You were in a pretty close place," I ventured.

" Close place, nothin'," he remarked in a tone of vast contempt. " Ye s'pose I wus goin' ter stan' 'roun' ther' er suckin' my thumb, like them dern niggers, an' not vote ? "

" But what could you do ? " I demanded.

" Do ? What 'd I do ? " he repeated, with a peculiar sardonic grin. " W'y, I jes' nat'ly grabbed thet constertootion an' read it for'd an' back'rds an' sideways an' edgeways, thet 's w'at I done; an' I 'splained ever single dern word o' it ter them jedges jes' like er loryer ter a jury. Vote? I cud er voted seving times ef I 'd wanted ter. An' nary dern nigger got er smell!"

I laughed, of course.

" Hit air sorter funny," he admitted, with a wink, " an' I s'pec' 'at I won't be able ter read er nother dad burn word tell nex' 'lection!"

Up in the true mountain country the negroes have never given any very great political trouble; but in a few localities, under stress of a particularly close and exciting squabble for office, the balance of power has been negatively, if not positively, controlled by the colored element. Curiously enough, the candidate who has gained this deciding increment has been invariably defeated ; nor is this rule likely to be changed in the future. The balance of power, like every other political gift accidentally tossed to the negroes by a grotesque fortune, is but a huge joke to be cracked on the color-line.

But notwithstanding the humor of these slowly fading conditions, the facts under them are grim, dense, imperishable; they demand respectful and unprejudiced treatment in art and history, as registering the vanishing-point of a tremendous old-time influence and the starting-point of a new régime in the hill country. What a period of romance the old slavery time was; and yet it had no romancer! What a life of poetry; but it had no poet! What a cycle of history; yet not a historian to record it! What an epic; and never a Homer! What a tragedy; but not a Sophocles, not a Shakespeare!

BEN AND JUDAS

On a dark and stormy summer night, early in the present century, two male children were born on the Wilson plantation in middle Georgia. One of the babes came into the world covered with a skin as black as the night, the other was of that complexion known as sandy; one was born a slave, the other a free American citizen. Two such screeching and squalling infants never before or since assaulted simultaneously the peace of the world. Such lungs had they, and such vocal chords, that cabin and mansion fairly shook with their boisterous and unrhythmical wailing. The white mother died, leaving her chubby, kicking, bawling offspring to share the breast of the more fortunate colored matron with the fat, black, howling

hereditary dependent thereto ; and so Ben
and Judas, master and slave, began their
companionship at the very fountain of life.
They grew, as it were, arm in arm and
quite apace with each other, as healthy
boys will, crawling, then toddling, anon
running on the sandy lawn between the
cabin and the mansion, often quarreling,
sometimes fighting vigorously.   Soon
enough, however, Judas discovered that,
by some invisible and inscrutable decree,
he was slave to Ben, and Ben became aware
that he was rightful master to Judas.   The
conditions adjusted themselves to the lives
of the boys in a most peculiar way.   The
twain became almost inseparable, and grew
up so intimately that Judas looked like the
black shadow of Ben.   If one rode a horse,
the other rode a mule; if the white boy
habitually set his hat far back on his head,
the negro did the same; if Ben went swim-
ming or fishing, there went Judas also.
And yet Ben was forever scolding Judas

and threatening to whip him, a proceeding
treated quite respectfully and as a matter
of course by the slave. Wherever they
went Ben walked a pace or two in advance
of Judas, who followed, however, with exactly the consequential air of his master,
and with a step timed to every peculiarity
observable in the pace set by his leader.
Ben's father, who became dissipated and
careless after his wife's death, left the boy
to come up rather loosely, and there was
no one to make a note of the constantly
growing familiarity between the two youths;
nor did any person chance to observe how
much alike they were becoming as time
slipped away. Ben's education was neg-
lected, albeit now and again a tutor was
brought to the Wilson place, and some effort was made to soften the crust of ignorance which was forming around the lad's
mind. Stormy and self-willed, with a peculiar facility in the rapid selection and
instantaneous use of the most picturesque

and outlandish expletives, Ben drove these adventurous disciples of learning one by one from the place, and at length grew to manhood and to be master of the Wilson plantation (when his father died) without having changed in the least the manner of his life. He did not marry, nor did he think of marriage, but grew stout and round-shouldered, stormed and raved when he felt like it, threatened all the negroes, whipped not one of them, and so went along into middle life, and beyond, with Judas treading as exactly as possible in his footprints.

They grew prematurely old, these two men : the master's white hair was matched by the slave's snowy wool ; they both walked with a shuffling gait, and their faces gradually took on a network of wrinkles ; neither wore any beard. To this day it remains doubtful which was indebted most to the other in the matter of borrowed characteristics. The negro

hoarded up the white man's words, especially the polysyllabic ones, and in turn the
white man adopted in an elusive, modified
way the negro's pronunciation and gestures. If the African apostatized and fell
away from the grace of a savage taste to
like soda biscuits and very sweet coffee,
the American of Scotch descent dropped
so low in barbarity that he became a confirmed 'possum-eater. Ben Wilson could
read after a fashion, and had a taste for
romance of the swashbuckler, kidnap-a-
heroine sort. Judas was a good listener,
as his master mouthed these wonderful
stories aloud, and his hereditary Congo
imagination, crude but powerful, was fed
and strengthened by the pabulum thus
absorbed.

It was a picture worth seeing, worth
sketching in pure colors and setting in an
imperishable frame, that group, the master,
the slave, and the dog Chawm. Chawm is
a name boiled down from " chew them ; "

as a Latin commentator would put it:
chew them, *vel* chaw them, *vel* chaw 'em,
vel chawm. He was a copperas-yellow cur
of middle size and indefinite age, who loved
to lie at the feet of his two masters and
snap at the flies. This trio, when they
came together for a literary purpose, usually occupied that part of the old vine-cov-
ered veranda which caught the black afternoon shade of the Wilson mansion. In
parenthesis let me say that I use this word
mansion out of courtesy, for the house was
small and dilapidated; the custom of the
country made it a mansion, just as Ben
Wilson was made Colonel Ben.

There they were, the white, the black,
and the dog, enjoying a certain story of
mediæval days, about a nameless, terrible
knight-errant who had stolen and borne
away the beautiful Rosamond; and about
the slender, graceful youth who buckled
his heavy armor on to ride off in melodramatic pursuit. Judas listened with

eyes half closed and mouth agape ; Chawm
was panting, possibly with excitement, his
red tongue lolling and weltering, and his
kindly brown eyes upturned to watch the
motions of Ben's leisurely lips.   There was
a wayward breeze, a desultory satin rustle,
in the vine-leaves.   The sky was cloudless,
the red country road hot and dusty, the
mansion all silent within.   Some negro
ploughmen were singing plaintively far off
in a cornfield.   The eyes of Judas grew
blissfully heavy, closed themselves, his
under jaw fell lower, he snored in a deep,
mellow, well-satisfied key.   Ben ceased
reading and looked at the sleepers, for
Chawm, too, had fallen into a light doze.

"Dad blast yer lazy hides! Wake erp
yer, er I 'll thrash ye till ye don't know yer-
selves! Wake up, I say!" Ben's voice
started echoes in every direction.   Chawm
sprung to his feet, Judas caught his breath
with an inward snort and started up, glaring inquiringly at his raging master.

"Yer jes' go to that watermillion patch and git to yer hoein' of them vines mighty fast, er I'll whale enough hide off'm yer to half-sole my boots, yer lazy, good-fer-nothin', low-down, sleepy-headed, snorin', flop-yeared"— He hesitated, rummaged in his memory for yet another adjective. Meantime, Judas had scrambled up unsteadily, and was saying, "Yah sah, yah sah," as fast as ever he could, and bowing apologetically while his hands performed rapid deprecatory gestures.

"Move off, I say!" thundered Ben.

Chawm, with his tail between his legs, followed Judas, who went in search of his hoe, and soon after the negro was heard singing a camp-meeting song over in the melon patch:—

> "Ya-a-as, my mother's over yander,
> Ya-a-as, my mother's over yander,
> Ya-a-as, my mother's over yander,
> On de oder sho'."

To any casual observer who for a series

of years had chanced now and again to see
these twain, it must have appeared that
Ben Wilson's chief aim in life was to
storm at Judas, and that Judas, not daring
to respond in kind directly to the voluble
raging of his master, lived for the sole purpose of singing religious songs and heap-
ing maledictions on Bolus, his mule. If
Ben desired his horse saddled and brought
to him, he issued the order somewhat as
follows : —

"Judas ! Hey there, ye ole hump-
backed scamp ! How long air ye a-goin'
to be a-fetchin' me that hoss ? Hurry up !
Step lively, er I 'll tie ye up an' jest whale
the whole skin off'm ye ! Trot lively, I
say ! "

Really, what did Judas care if Ben spoke
thus to him? The master never had struck
the slave in anger since the days when
they enjoyed the luxury of their childish
fisticuffs. These threats were the merest
mouthing, and Judas knew it very well.

" Yah, dar! Yo' Bolus! yo' ole rib-nosed, so'-eyed, knock-kneed, pigeon-toed t'ief! I jes' wa' yo' out wid er fence-rail, ef yo' don' step pow'ful libely now; sho 's yo' bo'n I jest will ! "

This was the echo sent back from the rickety stables by Judas to the ears of his master, who sat smoking his short pipe on the sunken veranda under his vine and close to his gnarled fig-tree. The voice was meant to sound very savage; but in spite of Judas it would be melodious and unimpressive, a mere echo and nothing more, — *vox, et præterea nihil.*

Ben always chuckled reflectively when he heard Judas roaring like that. He could not have said just why he chuckled; perhaps it was mere force of habit.

" Dad blast that fool nigger ! " he would mutter below his breath. " Puts me in mind of a hongry mule a-brayin' fer fodder. I 'll skin 'im alive fer it yet."

" Confoun' Mars' Ben ! Better keep he

ole mouf shet," Judas would growl; but neither ever heard the side remarks of the other. Indeed, in a certain restricted and abnormal way they were very tender of each other's feelings. The older they grew the nearer came these two men together. It was as if, setting out from widely separated birthrights, they had journeyed towards the same end, and thus, their paths converging, they were at last to lie down in graves dug side by side.

But no matter if their cradle was a common one, and notwithstanding that their footsteps kept such even time, Ben was master, Judas slave. They were differentiated at this one point, and at another, the point of color, irrevocably, hopelessly. As other differences were sloughed; as atom by atom their lines blended together; as strange attachments, like the feelers of vines, grew between them; and as the license of familiarity took possession of them more and more, the attitude of the

master partook of tyranny in a greater degree. I use the word "attitude," because
it expresses precisely my meaning. Ben
Wilson's tyranny was an attitude, nothing
more. Judas never had seen the moment
when he was afraid of his master; still,
there was a line over which he dared not
step — the line of downright disobedience.
In some obscure way the negro felt the
weakness of the white man's character,
from which a stream of flashing, rumbling
threats had poured for a lifetime; he knew
that Ben Wilson was a harmless blusterer,
who was scarcely aware of his own windy
utterances, and yet he hesitated to admit
that he knew it — nay, he forced himself
to be proud of his master's prodigious tem-
peramental expansions. He felt his own
importance in the world barely below that
of the man who owned him, and deep in
his old heart stirred the delicious dream of
freedom. What a dream! Amorphous as
a cloud, and rosy as ever morning vapor

was, it informed his soul with vague, haunting perfumes and nameless strains of song. Strange that so crude a being could absorb such an element into the innermost tissues of his life! Judas had a conscience, rudimentary indeed, but insistent, which gnawed him frightfully at times; not for stealing, — he was callous to that, — but for rebellion, which he could not cast out of him entirely. Occasionally he soliloquized: —

"Ef I could jest be de mars' erwhile an' Mars' Ben be de nigger, bress de good Lor', but would n't I jest mor' 'n mek 'im bounce erroun' one time! Sorty fink I 'd wake 'im up afore day, an' would n't I cuss 'im an' 'buse 'im an' rah an' cha'ge at 'im tell he know 'zactly how it was hese'f! Yo' may say so, honey, dat yo' may!"

Following treasonable thoughts like these came bitings by the hot teeth of the poor slave's conscience, all the deeper and crueler by contrast with the love forever upgushing to be lavished on his truly indulgent, but strongly exasperating master.

"Lor', do forgib po' ole Judas," he would pray, "kase he been er jokin' ter he-se'f 'bout er pow'ful ticklish ci'cumstance, sho''s yo' bo'n, Lor'; an' he no business trompin' roun' er ole well in de night. Git he neck broke, sho'!"

Notwithstanding conscience and prayer, however, the thought grew clearer and waxed more vigorous in the heart of Judas as the years slipped by and Ben gradually increased his scolding. The more he fought it the closer clung to him the vision of that revolution which would turn him on top and Ben below, if but for a few moments of delirious triumph.

"Lor', but would n't Mars' Ben hate 'r hab dis ole nigger er cha'gin' an' er rantin' an' er yellin' at 'im, an' jest er cussin' 'im like de berry debil fo' eberyt'ing 'at 's mean, an' de sweat jest er rollin' off 'm, an' 'im jest eberlastin'ly an' outlandishly er

gibbin' 'im de limmer jaw fo' he laziness
an' he dog-gone general no 'countness!
Ef dat would n't be satisfactionel ter dis
yer darkey, den I dunno nuffin' 't all 'bout
it. Dat's his way er doin' me, an' it seem
lak my time orter be comin' erlong poorty
soon ter do 'im dat er way er leetle, debil
take de nigger ef it don't!"

In good truth, however, Judas had no
right to complain of hard work; he did
not earn his salt. A large part of the time
he and his master occupied with angling
in the rivulet hard by, wherein catfish were
the chief game. Side by side on the sandy
bank of the stream the twain looked like
two frogs ready to leap into the water, so
expectant and eager were their wrinkled
faces and protruding eyes; so comically
set akimbo their arms and legs. With
little art they cast and recast their clumsy
bait of bacon-rind, exchanging few words,
but enjoying, doubtless, a sense of subtile
companionship peculiarly satisfying.

SIDE BY SIDE ON THE SANDY BANK OF THE STREAM

" Airy a bite, Judas ? "

" No, sah."

" Too lazy to keep yer hook baited ? "

" No, sah."

A while of silence, the river swashing dreamily, the sunshine shimmering far along the slowly lapsing current; then Judas begins humming a revival tune.

"Shet yer mouth; stop that infernal howling, yer blasted old eejit, er I 'll take this yer fish-pole an' I 'll nat'rally lam the life out of ye ! " storms the master. " Ye 'll scare all the fish till they 'll go clean to the Gulf of Mexico. Hain't ye got a triffin' of sense left ? "

The slave sulks in silence. Ten minutes later Ben takes out a plug of bright, greasy-looking navy tobacco, and after biting off a liberal chew says in a very soft voice : —

" Here, Jude, try some of my tobacker, an' maybe yer luck 'll change."

Judas fills his cheek with the comforting weed and gazes with expectant con-

tentment into the stream, but the luck con-
tinues much the same. The wind may
blow a trifle sweeter, fluting an old Pan-
pipe tune in a half-whisper through the
fringe of shining reeds, and the thrushes
may trill suddenly a strange, soft phrase
from the dark foliage of the grove hard by;
still, in blissful ignorance of the voices of
nature and all unaware of their own picturesqueness, without a nibble to encour-
age them, the two white-haired men watch
away the golden afternoon. At last, just
as Judas has given up and is winding his
line around his pole, Ben yanks out a
slimy, wriggling, prickly catfish, and his
round face flings forth through its screen
of wrinkles a spray of sudden excitement.

" Grab 'im, Judas! Grab 'im, ye lubberly
old lout ye! What ye doin' a-grinnin' an'
a-gazin' an' that fish a-floppin' right back
— grab 'im! If ye do let 'im get away, I 'll
break yer old neck an' pull out yer backbone — grab 'im, I say! "

Judas scrambles after the fish, sprawling and grabbing, while it actively flops about in the sand. It spears him cruelly till the red blood is spattered over his great rusty black hands, but he captures it finally and puts a stick through its gills.

On many and many an afternoon they trudged homeward together in the softening light, Judas carrying both rods on his shoulder, the bait-cups in his hands, and the string of fish, if there were any, dangling somewhere about his squat person. The black man might have been the incarnate shadow of the white one, so much were they alike in everything but color. Even to a slight limp of the left leg, their movements were the same. Each had a peculiar fashion of setting his right elbow at a certain angle, and of elevating slightly the right shoulder. Precisely alike sat their well-worn straw hats far over on the back of their heads.

It was in the spring of 1860 that Ben

took the measles and came near to death.
Judas nursed his master with a faithfulness
that knew not the shadow of abatement
until the disease had spent its force and
Ben began to convalesce. With the turn
of the tide which bore him back from the
shore of death the master recovered his
tongue, and grew refractory and abusive in-
versely as the negro was silent and obedi-
ent. He exhausted upon poor Judas, over
and over again, the vocabulary of vitupera-
tive epithets at his command. When Ben
was quite well Judas lay down with the
disease.

"A nigger with the measles! Well, I'll
be dern! Ye're gone, Jude,— gone fer
sure. Measles nearly always kills a nigger,
an' ye mought es well begin ter wall up
yer eyes an' wiggle yer toes."

Ben uttered these consoling words as he
entered his old slave's cabin and stood beside the low bed. "Not much use ter do
anythin' fer ye's I know of — bound ter

go this time.   Don't ye feel a sort of dyin'
sensation in yer blamed old bones already?"

But Judas was nursed by his master as
a child by its mother.   Never was man
better cared for night and day.   Ben's
whole life for the time was centred in the
one thought of saving the slave.   In this
he was absolutely unselfish and at last
successful.

As Judas grew better, after the crisis
was passed, he did not fail to follow his
master's example and make himself as
troublesome as possible.   Nothing was
good enough for him; none of his food
was properly prepared or served, his bed
was not right, he wanted water from a certain distant spring, he grumbled at Ben
without reason, and grew more abusive
and personal daily.   At last, one afternoon
Ben came out of the cabin with a very
peculiar look on his face.   He stopped as
he left the threshold, and with his hands in

his trousers' pockets and his head thrown back he whistled a low, gentle note.

"Well, I'll everlastin'ly jest be dad burned!" he exclaimed. Then he puffed out his wrinkled cheeks till they looked like two freckled bladders. "Who'd 'a' thought it!" He chuckled long and low, looking down at his boots and then up at the sky. "Cussed me! Cussed me! The blame old rooster a-cussin' me! Don't seem possible, but he did all the same. Gamest nigger I ever seen!"

It must have been a revelation to the master when the old slave actually swore at him and cursed him vigorously. Ben went about chuckling retrospectively and muttering to himself: —

"The old coon he cussed me!"

Next day for dinner Judas had chicken pie and dumplings, his favorite pot, and Ben brought some old peach brandy from the cellar and poured it for him with his own hands.

In due time the negro got well and the two resumed their old life, a little feebler, a trifle more stoop in their shoulders, their voices huskier, but yet quite as happy as before.

The watermelon - patch has ever been the jewel on the breast of the Georgia plantation. "What is home without a watermelon?" runs the well-known phrase, and in sooth what cool, delicious suggestions run with it! Ben and Judas each had a patch, year in and year out. Not that Ben ever hoed in his; but he made Judas keep it free of weeds. Here was a source of trouble; for invariably the negro's patch was better, the melons were the larger and finer. Scold and storm and threaten as he might, Ben could not change this, nor could he convince his slave that there was anything at all strange in the matter.

"How I gwine fin' out 'bout what mek yo' watermillions so runty an' so scrunty?" Judas exclaimed. "Hain't I jest hoed 'em

an' ploughed 'em an' took care ob em an'
try ter mek 'em do somefin'? But dey jest
kinder wommux an' squommux erlong an'
don't grow wof er dern! I jest sw'a' I
can't holp it, Mars' Ben, ef yo' got no luck
erbout yo' nohow! Watermillions grows
ter luck, not ter de hoe."

"Luck! Luck!" bawled Ben, shaking
his fist at the negro. "Luck! yer old
lump er lamp-black — yer old, lazy, sneakin'
scamp! I'll show ye about luck! Ef I
don't have a good patch of watermillions
next year I'll skin ye alive, see ef I don't,
ye old villain ye!"

It was one of Ben's greatest luxuries to
sit on the top rail of the worm-fence which
inclosed the melon-patch, his own particular patch, and superintend the hoeing
thereof. To Judas this was a bitter ordeal,
and its particular tang grew more offensive
year by year, as the half-smothered longing
to be master, if but for a moment, gripped
his imagination closer and closer.

"Ef I jest could set up dah on dat fence an' cuss 'im while he hoed, an' ef I jest could one time see 'im er hus'lin' erroun' w'en I tole 'im, dis nigger 'd be ready ter die right den. Lor', I'd give it to 'im good!"

Any observer a trifle sharper than Ben would have read Judas's thoughts as he ruminated thus; but Ben was not a student of human nature, — or, for that matter, any other nature,—and he scolded away merely to give vent to the pressure of habit.

One morning, when the melon vines were young, — it must have been late in April, — Judas leaned on his hoe-handle, and looking up at Ben, who sat on the fence top, as usual, smoking his short pipe, he remarked:—

"Don' ye yer dat mockin'-bird er tee-diddlin' an' er too-doodlin', Mars' Ben?"

"I'll tee-diddle an' too-doodle ye, ef ye don't keep on a-hoein'," raged Ben. "This year I'm bound ter have some big melons, ef I have ter wear ye out ter do it!"

Judas sprung to work, and for about a minute hoed desperately; then looking up again he said, "De feesh allus bites bestest w'en de mockin'-birds tee-diddles an' too-doodles dat way."

Such a flood of abusive eloquence as Ben now let go upon the balmy morning air would have surprised and overwhelmed a less adequately fortified soul than that of Judas. The negro, however, was well pre-pared for the onslaught, and received it with most industrious though indifferent silence. When the master had exhausted both his breath and his vocabulary, the negro turned up his rheumy eyes and sug-gested that "feesh ain't gwine ter bite eber' day like day 'll bite ter-day." This remark was made in a tone of voice expressive of absent-mindedness, and almost instantly the speaker added dreamily, leaning on his hoe again : —

" Time do crawl off wid a feller's life pow'ful fast, Mars' Ben. Seem lak yistyd'y,

or day 'foer yistyd'y, 'at we 's leetle beety
boys. Don' yo' 'member w'en ole Bolus
— dat fust Bolus, I mean — done went an'
kick de lof' outer de new stable? We 's er
gittin' pooty ole, Mars' Ben, pooty ole, ain't
we ? "

"Yea, an' we 'll die an' be buried an'
resurrected, ye old vagabond ye, before ye
get one hill of this here patch hoed!"
roared Ben. Judas did not move, but, wagging his head in a dreamy way, said : —

"I 'members one time" — here he chuckled softly — "I 'members one time w'en
we had er fight an' I whirped yo'; made
yo' yelp out an' say ''Nough, 'nough!
Take 'im off!' an' Moses, how I wus er
linkin' it ter yo' wid bof fists ter onct! Dose
yo' rickermember dat, Mars' Ben ?"

Ben remembered. It was when they
were little children, before Judas had found
out his hereditary limitation, and before
Ben had dreamed of asserting the supe-
riority inherent in his blood. Somehow

the retrospect filled the master's vision instantly with a sort of Indian-summer haze of tenderness. He forgot to scold. For some time there was silence, save that the mocking-bird poured forth a song as rich and plaintive as any ever heard by Sappho under the rose-bannered garden walls of Mitylene; then Judas, with sudden energy, exclaimed: —

" Mars' Ben, yo' nebber did whirp me, did yo'? "

Ben, having lapsed into retrospective distance, did not heed the negro's interrogation, but sat there on the fence with his pipe-stem clamped between his teeth. He was smiling in a mild, childish way.

" No," added Judas, answering his own question — " no, yo' nebber whirped me in yo' life; but I whirped yo' onct like de berry debil, did n't I, Mars' Ben ? "

Ben's hat was far back on his head, and his thin, white hair shone like silver floss on his wrinkled forehead, — the expression of his face that of silly delight in a barren and commonplace reminiscence.

"Mars' Ben, I wants ter ax one leetle fabor ob yo'."

The master clung to his distance and his dream.

"Hey dar! Mars' Ben!"

"Well, what yer want, yer old scare-crow?" inquired Ben, pulling himself to-gether and yawning so that he dropped his pipe, which Judas quickly restored to him.

"Well, Mars' Ben, 't ain't much w'at I wants, but I 's been er wantin' it seem lak er thousan' years."

Ben began to look dreamy again.

"I wants ter swap places wid yo', Mars' Ben, dat 's w'at I wants," continued Judas, speaking rapidly, as if forcing out the words against heavy pressure of restraint. "I wants ter set up dah on dat fence, an' yo' git down yer an' I cuss yo', an' yo' jest hoe like de debil — dat's w'at I wants."

It was a slow process by which Judas at

last forced upon his master's comprehen-
sion the preposterous proposition for a
temporary exchange of situations. Ben
could not understand it fully until it had
been insinuated into his mind particle by
particle, so to speak; for the direct method
failed wholly, and the wily old African
resorted to subtile suggestion and elusive
supposititious illustration of his desire.

"We's been er libin' tergedder lo! des
many ye'rs, Mars' Ben, an' did I eber 'fuse
ter do anyfing 'at yo' axed me? No, sah,
I neber did. Sort er seem lak yo' mought
do jest dis one leetle 'commodation fo'
me."

Ben began to grin in a sheepish, half-
fascinated way as the proposition gradually
took hold of his imagination. How would
it feel to be a "nigger" and have a master
over him? What sort of sensation would
it afford to be compelled to do implicitly
the will of another, and that other a querulous and conscienceless old sinner like

Judas? The end of it was that he slid down from his perch and took the hoe, while Judas got up and sat on the fence.

"Han' me dat pipe," was the first peremptory order.

Ben winced, but gave up the coveted nicotian censer.

"Now, den, yo' flop-yeared, bandy-shanked, hook nosed, freckle-faced, wall-eyed, double-chinned, bald-headed, hump-shoul'ered " —

"Come, now, Judas," Ben interrupted, " I won't stan' no sech langwidges " —

"Hol' on dah, Mars' Ben," cried Judas in an injured tone. "Yo' p'omised me yo''d do it, an' I knows yo''s not gwine back on yo' wo'd; no Wilson eber do dat."

Ben was abashed. It was true no Wilson ever broke a promise. The Wilsons were men of honor.

"Well, fire away," he said, falling to work again. " Fire away!"

"Hussle up, dah! Hussle up, yo' lazy

ole vagabon' yo', er I 'll git down f'om heah, an' I 'll w'ar out ebery hic'ry sprout in de county on yo' ole rusty back! Git erlong! — hurry up! — faster! Don' yo' heah? Ef I do come down dah I 'll jes' nat'rally comb yo' head tell ebery ha'r on it 'll sw'ar de day ob judgment done come! I 'll wa'm yo' jacket tell de dus' er comin' out'n it 'll look lak a sto'm-cloud! Wiggle faster, er I 'll yank out yo' backbone an' mek er trace-chain out'n it! Don' yo' heah me, Ben?"

Ben heard and obeyed. Never did hoe go faster, never was soil so stirred and pulverized. The sweat sprung from every pore of the man's skin, it trickled over his face and streamed from his chin, it saturated his clothes.

Judas was intoxicated with delight; almost delirious with the sensation of freedom and masterhood. His eloquence increased as the situation affected his imagination, and his words tumbled forth

in torrents. Not less was Ben absorbed
and carried away. He was a slave, Judas
was his master, the puppet must wriggle
when the owner pulled the strings. He
worked furiously. Judas forgot to smoke
the pipe, but held it in his hand and made
all sorts of gestures with it.

"Hit dem clods! Mash 'em fine!" he
screamed. "Don' look up, yo' ole poky
tarrypin yo'! Ef yo' does I 'll wommux de
hide off'm yo' blamed ole back faster 'n
forty-seben shoemakers kin peg it on ag'in!
Hussle, I tole yo', er I 'll jest wring yo'
neck an' tie yo' years in er hard knot! Yo'
heah me now, Ben?"

This was bad enough, but not the worst,
for Judas used many words and phrases
not permissible in print. He spared no
joint of his master's armor, he left no vul-
nerable point unassailed. The accumulated
riches of a lifetime spent in collecting a picturesque vocabulary, and the stored force
of nearly sixty years given to private prac-

tice in using it, now served him a full turn.
In the thickest shower of the negro's
mingled threats, commands, and maledictions, however, Ben quit work, and, leaning
on his hoe, panted rapidly.   He gazed up
at Judas pathetically and said : —

" How that mockin'-bird does tee-diddle
an' too-doodle ! "

Judas actually stopped short in the mid
career of his eloquence, and Ben added : —

" Never see sich signs for feesh a-bitin';
did you, Judas ? "

The charm was broken, the farce was
ended.   A little later the two old men
might have been seen with their bait-cups
and fishing-poles in their hands toddling
along down the slope to the rivulet, the
white leading, the black following.   They
were both rather abstracted, it appeared,
for each cast in his hook without any
bacon rind on it, and sat on the stream's
bank all the rest of the forenoon in blissful
expectancy of an impossible nibble.

One good came of the little episode at the melon-patch. The vine around whose roots Ben had plied the hoe with such vigor thrived amazingly, and in due time bore a watermelon of huge size, a grand spheroid as green as emerald and as richly soft in surface color as the most costly old velvet.

"Got de twin ob it down dah in my patch," said Judas; " jest es much like it es one bean 's like anoder bean. Yo' orter come down an' see it, Mars Ben."

Ben went, and sure enough, there was a melon just the duplicate of his own. Of course, however, he claimed that he saw some indices of inferiority in Judas's fruit, but he could n't just point them out — possibly the rind was not as healthy-looking, he thought, and then the stem appeared to be shriveling. Judas, for his part, was quite sure that his master's melon would not "sweeten up" as his would, and that it would be found lacking in the "jawlee-

ciousness " and that " fo'-de-Lor'-sake-hand-
me-some-moreness " so characteristic of
those of his own raising.

Ben's pride in his melon matured and
ripened at the same time with the maturing
and ripening of that wonderful globule of
racy pulp and juice whose core he longed
to see. After so many failures, here at last
was his triumph. There was a certain danger connected with plucking this melon.
It was of a variety locally called "ice-rind"
on account of the thickness of the outer
part or shell which made it very difficult to
know when it was ripe, and so Ben dreaded
to act. Every evening in the latest dusk
of twilight he would go out and lean over
the patch fence to have a darkling view of
his treasure, which thus seen was mightily
magnified.

When the moment of sacrifice had come,
Ben actually shrunk from the task of plucking that melon. He leaned on the fence
until it was quite dark and until the moon

had begun to show in the east before he bethought him that that night was Judas's birth-night, and then a bright idea came to him. He would take the melon to the old slave's cabin and they would have a feast. But when he had climbed over the fence and had stooped above the huge dusky sphere, his heart failed him, and at the same time another thought struck him with great force. He straightened himself up, placed his hands on his hips, and chuckled. Just the thing! The best joke on Judas! He would go to the negro's patch, steal his big melon, and share it with him on the following day.

His own melon he would keep a few days longer to be sure that it had ripened. A very simple proceeding, without a thought of dishonor in it.

It was as beautiful and balmy a midsummer night as ever fell upon the world. Ben felt its soft influence in his old blood as he toddled surreptitiously along the path leading through a little wood to Judas's cabin and patch. He was picturing in his mind how foolish Judas would look and how beaten he would feel when he found out that he had been feasting on his own big melon. One might have seen by the increasing light of the moon that Ben's trelliswork of facial wrinkles could scarcely hold in the laughing glee that was in him, and his eyes twinkled while his mouth drew itself on to a set, suppressed smile. Chawm trotted along silently at Ben's heels, his tail drooping and his ears hanging limp. In the distance, amid the hills, an owl was hooting dolefully, but the little wood was as silent as the grave. Suddenly Ben heard a footfall coming up the path, and he slipped into the bushes just in time to let Judas go shuffling by all unaware.

"The blamed old rooster," he said to himself in a tender, affectionate whisper. "The blamed old rooster! I wonder what he's a-thinkin' about jest now?"

Chawm slipped out and fell noiselessly behind Judas, following him on towards the mansion. Ben chuckled with deep satisfaction as he climbed over into Judas's patch and laid hands on the negro's large melon. What a typical thief he appeared as he hurried furtively along, stooping low with his ill-gotten load, his crooked shadow dancing vaguely beside him! Over the fence he toiled with difficulty, the melon was so heavy and slippery; then along the path. Once in the shadowy wood, he laid down his burden and wiped his dewy face with his sleeve. He did not realize how excited he was; it was the first time in all his life that he had ever stolen anything even in fun. Every little sound startled him and made him pant. He felt as if running as fast as his legs could carry him would be the richest of all luxuries.

When again he picked up the melon and resumed his way he found his heart fluttering and his limbs weak, but he hurried on.

Suddenly he halted, with a black apparition barring the path before him.

" Judas! you old coon!"

" Mars' Ben!"

They leaned forward and glared at each other.

" Mars' Ben! Yo' been er stealin' my watermillion!"

" Judas! You thieven' old rooster! You 've stole " —

Their voices blended, and such a mixture! The wood resounded. They stood facing each other, as much alike as duplicates in everything save color, each clasping in his arms the other's watermelon. It was a moment of intense surprise, of voluble swearing, of picturesque posturing; then followed a sudden collapse and down fell both great, ripe, luscious spheres with a dull, heavy bump, breaking open on the ground and filling the air with a spray of sweet juice and the faint luxuriant aroma so dear to Georgian nostrils. Chawm stepped forward and sniffed idly and indifferently at one of the pieces. A little screech-owl mewed plaintively in the bush hard by. Both men, having exhausted themselves simultaneously, began to sway and tremble, their legs slowly giving way under them. The spot of moonlight in which they stood lent a strange effect to their bent and faltering forms. Judas had been more or less a thief all his life, but this was the first time he had ever been caught in the act, therefore he was as deeply shocked as was Ben. Down they sank until they sat flat on the ground in the path and facing each other, the broken melons between them. Chawm took position a little to one side and looked on gravely, as if he felt the solemnity of the occasion.

Judas was first to speak.

"Well, I jest be 'sentially an' eberlast-in'ly "—

"Shet up!" stormed Ben.

They looked sheepishly at each other, while Chawm licked his jaws with perfunctory nonchalance. After what seemed a very long silence, Ben said: —

" Jude, ax a blessin' afore we eats."

Judas hesitated.

" Did ye hear what I was a-sayin' for yer to do? " inquired Ben. " Ax a blessin', I say!" The negro bowed his old snow-fleeced head and prayed: —

"Lor', hab mercy on two ole villyans an' w'at dey done steal f'om one 'nudder. Spaycially, Lor', forgib Mars' Ben, kase he rich an' free an' he orter hab mo' honah 'bout 'im 'an ter steal f'om po' nigger. I used to fink, Lor', dat Mars' Ben 's er mighty good man, but seem lack yer lately he gittin' so on'ry 'at yo' 'll be erbleeged ter hannel 'im pooty sabage ef he keep on. Dey may be 'nough good lef' in 'im ter pay fer de trouble ob foolin' 'long wid 'im, but hit 's pow'ful doubtful, an' dat 's er fac'. Lor', I don't advise yo' ter go much outer

yo' way ter 'commodate sich er outdacious
old sneak-t'ief an' sich er "—

"Judas!" roared Ben, "yer jest stop
right now!"

"An' bress dese watermillions w'at we 's
erbout ter receib, amen!" concluded Judas.
"Try er piece er dis here solid core, Mars'
Ben; hit look mighty jawleecious."

And so there in the space of moonlight
they munched, with many watery mouth-
ings, the sweet central hearts of the pil-
fered fruit. All around them the birds
stirred in their sleep, rustling the leaves
and letting go a few dreamy chirps. Overhead a great rift uncovered the almost
purple sky.

They did not converse while they were
eating, but when the repast was ended Judas apologized and explained in their joint
behalf: —

"Yo' see, Mars' Ben, I 's yo' nigger an'
yo' 's my marster. W'at 's yo's is mine, an'
w'at 's mine 's yo's; see? an' hit ain't no

mo' harm 'an nothin' fo' us ter steal f'om one 'nudder. Lor', Mars' Ben, I been er knowin' all my life 'at I was er stealin' f'om yo'; but I nebber dream 'at it was yo' 'at was er takin' all er my bestest watermillions an' t'ings. 'Spec' we 's 'bout eben now, Mars' Ben. Ef yo 's a leetle bit ahead ob me I 's not er keerin'; hit 's all right."

So they wiped their mouths and parted for the night.

" Good-night, Mars' Ben."

" Good-night, Judas."

It would be cruel to follow them farther down the road of life, for rheumatism came, and then the war. Many an afternoon the trio, Ben, Judas, and Chawm, sat on the old veranda and listened to the far-off thunder of battle, not fairly realizing its meaning, but feeling that in some vague way it meant a great deal. After war, peace. After peace, reconstruction. After reconstruction, politics. Somebody took the trouble to insist upon having Ben Wilson go to

the polls and vote.   Of course Judas went
with him.   What a curious looking twain
they were, tottering along, almost side by
side now, their limbs trembling and their
eyes nearly blind !

"Got yer ticket, Jude?" inquired Ben.

"No, sah, dat's all right.   Yo' jest drap
one in, hit 'll do fo' bofe ob us," answered
Judas.   And it was done.

They died a year ago.   Their graves
are side by side, and so close together that
a single slab might serve to cover them
both.   If I were rich it should be an imperishable monument, inscribed simply: —

BEN AND JUDAS,
AET. SEVENTY YEARS, ONE MONTH, AND FOURTEEN
DAYS.

HODSON'S HIDE-OUT

WHERE the great line of geologic upheaval, running down from Virginia
through North Carolina, Tennessee, and
Georgia, finally breaks up into a hopeless
confusion of variously trending ridges and
spurs, there is a region of country somewhat north of the centre of Alabama, called
by the inhabitants thereof "The Sand
Mounting." It is a wild, out-of-the way,
little-known country, whose citizens have
kept alive in their mountain fastnesses
nearly all that backwoods simplicity and
narrowness of ambition peculiar to their
ancestors, who came mostly from the Carolinas, in the early part of the present century, following the mountain lines in their
migrations, as fish follow streams. They
are honest and virtuous, as mountain folk

usually are, rather frugal and simple than industrious and enterprising, knowing nothing of books, and having very indefinite information touching the doings of the great world whose tides of action foam around their mountain-locked valleys like an ocean around some worthless island. They have heard of railroads, but many of them have never seen one. They do not take newspapers, they turn their backs upon missionaries, and they nurse a high disdain for the clothes and ways of city folk. Most of them are farmers in a small way, raising a little corn and wheat, a " patch " of cotton now and then, a few vegetables, and a great deal of delicious fruit.

In the days of secession the men of Sand Mountain were not zealous in the Southern cause, nor were they, on the other hand, willing to do battle for the Union. So it happened that when the Confederate authorities began a system of conscription, Sand Mountain was not a healthful place for enrolling officers, many of whom never returned therefrom to report the number of eligible men found in remote valleys and " Pockets."

One citizen of the mountain became notorious, if not strictly famous, during the war. His name was Riley Hodson, better known as Gineral Hodson, though he had never been a soldier. He may have been rather abnormally developed to serve as a representative Sand Mountain figure in this or any other sketch of that region. The reader may gather from the following outlines of Hodson's character, drawn by certain of his neighbors, a pretty fair idea of what the picture would be when filled out and properly shaded and lighted.

" Gineral Hodson air not jest ezactly what ye 'd call a contrary man, but he 's a mighty p'inted an' a orful sot in 'is way sort o' a feller," said Sandy Biddle, who stood six feet two in his home-made shoes, and weighed scarcely one hundred and twenty pounds, " an' ef anybody air enjoyin' any oncommon desire for a fight, he may call on the gineral with a reas'nable expectation of a-ketchin' double-barrel thunder an' hair-trigger lightnin'."

" He never hev be'n whirpt," observed old Ben Iley, himself the hero of some memorable rough-and-tumble fights, " an' he hev managed ter hev his own way, in spite o' 'ell an' high water, all over the mounting for mor' 'n forty year ter my sarting knowledge."

" When it come ter doctrin', es the scripter p'intedly do show it, he kin preach all round any o' yer meth'dist bible-bangers 'at ever I see, don't keer ef ye do call 'im a Hardshell an' a Forty-gallon, an' a' Iron-Jacket Baptus," was Wes Beasley's tribute; " an' I kin furder say," he added, cutting a quid from a twist of Sand Mountain tobacco and lodging it in his jaw, " 'at Gineral Hodson air hones', an' when he air a feller's frien' he air a good un, an' when he don't like ye, then hit air about time fer ye ter git up an' brin'le out'n the mounting."

Turning from these verbal sketches to look at Riley Hodson himself, we shall find him leaning on the rickety little gate in front of his rambling log house. In height he is six feet three, broad-shouldered, strong-limbed, rugged, grizzled, harsh-faced, unkempt. He looks like the embodiment of obstinacy. Nor is he out of place as a figure in the landscape around him. Nature was in no soft mood when she gave birth to Sand Mountain, and, in this particular spot, such labor as Riley Hodson had bestowed on its betterment had rendered the offspring more unsightly. Some yellowish clay fields, washed into ruts by the mountain rains, lay at all sorts of angles with the horizon; the fences were grown over with sassafras bushes and sour-grape vines, and there was as small evidence of any fertility of soil as there was of careful or even intelligent husbandry. It was in the spring of 1875, ten years after the close of the war, that Riley Hodson leaned on that gate and gazed up the narrow mountain trail at a man coming down.

" Hit air a peddler," he muttered to himself, taking the short-stemmed pipe from his mouth with a grimace of the most dogged dislike, — " hit air a peddler, an' ef them weeming ever git ther eyes sot onto 'im hit air good-by ter what money I hev on han', to a dead sartingty."

He opened the gate and passed through, going slowly along the trail to meet the coming stranger. Once or twice he glanced furtively back over his shoulder to see if his wife or daughter might chance to be looking after him from the door of the old house. He walked, in the genuine mountain fashion, with long, loose strides, his arms swinging awkwardly at his sides, and his head thrust forward, with his chin elevated and his shoulders drawn up. He

soon came face to face with a young man
of rather small stature and pleasing features, who carried a little pack on the end
of a short fowling-piece swung across his
left shoulder.

Hodson had made up his mind to drive
this young adventurer back, thinking him
an itinerant peddler; but a strange look
came into the old man's face, and he
stopped short with a half-frightened start
and a dumb gesture of awe and surprise.

The stranger, David D'Antinac by name,
and an ornithologist by profession, was a
little startled by this sudden apparition;
for Riley Hodson at best was not prepos-
sessing in appearance, and he glared so
strangely, and his face had such an ashy
pallor in it, that the strongest heart might
have shrunk and trembled at confronting
him in a lonely mountain trail.

"Well, ye blamed little rooster!" exclaimed Hodson in a breathless way, after
staring for a full minute.

D'Antinac recoiled perceptibly, with some show of excitement in his face. He was well aware that he was in a region not held well in hand by the law, and he had been told many wild tales of this part of Sand Mountain.

"Ye blamed little rooster!" repeated the old man, taking two or three short backward steps, as if half alarmed and half meditating a sudden leap upon D'Antinac, who now summoned voice enough to say :

" How do you do, sir ? "

Such a smile as one might cast upon the dead — a white, wondering, fearful smile — spread over Hodson's face. It seemed to D'Antinac that this smile even leaped from the face and ran like a ghastly flash across the landscape. He will remember it as long as he lives.

" W'y, Dave, er thet you ? " Hodson asked, in a harsh, tremulous tone, taking still another backward step.

" My name is certainly David, but I

guess you don't know me," said D'Antinac, with an effort at an easy manner.

"Don't know ye, ye pore little rooster!
Don't know ye! W'y, Dave, are ye come
ag'in?" The old man wavered and faltered, as if doubtful whether to advance or
retreat. "Don't know ye?" he repeated.
"W'y, Dave, don't *you* know *me?* Hev
ye furgot the ole man?"

"I beg your pardon, sir, but I believe I
never saw you before in my life," said
D'Antinac, lowering his little pack to the
ground and leaning on his gun. "You
are certainly laboring under some mistake."

"Never seed me afore!" cried Hodson,
his voice showing a rising belligerency.
"Ye blamed little rooster, none o' yer foolin', fer I won't stand it. I'll jes nat'rally
w'ar ye out ef ye come any o' that air."

Hodson now advanced a step or two
with threatening gestures. Quick as lightning, D'Antinac flung up his gun and
leveled it, his face growing very pale.

" Another step," he cried excitedly, " and I 'll shoot two holes through you ! "

Hodson stopped and said in a deprecating tone : —

" W'y, Dave, ye would n't shoot yer daddy, would ye, Dave ? "

" If *you* run onto me I 'll shoot *you*," was the firm response.

" W'y, ye blasted mean little rooster ! " thundered Hodson, and before D'Antinac in his excitement could pull trigger, the old man had him down and was sitting astride of him, as he lay at full length on his back. " Now I 'll jest nat'rally be dinged, Dave, ef I don't whirp ever' last striffin o' hide off'n ye ef ye don't erhave yerself ! " He had both of D'Antinac's arms clasped in one of his great hands, and was pressing them so hard against the young man's breast that he could scarcely breathe. " Ye nasty little rooster, a-comin' back an' a-tryin' ter shoot yer pore old daddy fer nothin'. I 'll jest wear ye out an' half-sole ye ag'in ef ye open yer mouth ! "

D'Antinac lay like a mouse under the paw of a lion. It was quite impossible for him to move. The old man's weight was enormous.

" I 'm er great notion ter pound the very daylights out'n ye afore I let ye up," Hodson continued. " Hit meks me mad 'nuff fer ter bite ye in two like er tater an' jest nat'rally chaw up both pieces, on'y ter think 'at ye 'd deny yer own daddy what 's larruped ye many a time, an' 'en try ter shoot 'im ! I 'm teetotally ershamed of ye, Dave. An' what 'll yer mammy say ? "

D'Antinac was possessed of a quick mind, and he had schooled it in the art of making the most of every exigency. He had been several years in the mountain regions of the South, and had discovered that the mountaineers liked nothing better than a certain sort of humor, liberally spiced with their peculiar slang.

"Speaking of biting a tater in two," he ejaculated rather breathlessly, "reminds me that I'm as hungry as a sitting hen. Have you got anything like a good mellow iron wedge or a fried pine-knot in your pocket?"

Hodson's face softened a little, and he smiled again, in that half ghastly way, as he said: —

"Ye dinged little rooster! W'y, Dave, der ye know the ole man now? Say, Dave, do ye?"

"Oh, yes, perfectly; never knew any one better in my life," promptly responded D'Antinac. "Your face is quite familiar, I assure you. How're the folks?"

Hodson chuckled deep down in his throat, at the same time somewhat relaxing his hold on the young man's arms.

"Sarah an' Mandy 'll jes nat'rally go 'stracted over ye, Dave, an' I want ye ter 'have yerself an' come wi' me down ter the house, like er white boy. This here foolin' 's not gwine ter do ye no good. Ye 've got to toe the mark, Dave."

"Oh, I'll behave," exclaimed D'Antinac. "I'll do whatever you want me to. I was only joking just now. Let me up; you're mashing me as flat as a flying-squirrel."

"Well, I don't whant ter hurt ye, but afore I ever let ye up, ye must promerse me one thing," said Hodson.

"What is it? Quick! for you are really making jelly of me," D'Antinac panted forth, like Encelados under Sicily.

"Thet ye'll not deny yer mammy ner Mandy; an' ef ye do deny 'em, I'll jest nat'rally be blamed ef I don't whale yer jacket tell ye won't know yer hide from a meal-sifter. Do ye promerse?"

"Yes," said D'Antinac, though in fact he did not understand the old mountaineer's meaning. The young man's mother had died in his babyhood, and he felt safe in promising never to deny her.

Hodson got up, leaving D'Antinac free

to rise; but the old fellow got possession of the gun and pack, and then said : —

"Now come 'long home, Dave, an' les' see what yer mammy an' Mandy 'll say ter ye. Come 'long, I say, an' don't stan' ther, a-gawpin' like er runt pig in er peach orchard. I do 'spise er fool. Come on, dad ding it, an' 'have yerself."

It is probable that no man was ever more bewildered than D'Antinac was just then; in fact, he could not command himself sufficiently to do more than stand there, after he had risen, and stupidly stare at Hodson. The latter, however, did not parley, but seizing one of the young man's arms in a vise-like grip, he began jerking him along the trail toward the house.

It was a subject fit for an artist's study, the old giant striding down the path, with the young man following at a trot. D'Antinac could not resist. He felt the insignificance of his physique, and also of his will, when compared with those of this old man of the mountain.

" I bet yer mammy 'll know ye, soon es she lays eyes onter ye, spite of yer new-fangled clo's an' yer fancy mustachers. An' es fur Mandy, don't s'pose she 'll 'member ye, case she wus too little w'en ye — w'en ye war' — w'en they tuck ye off. She was nothin' but er baby then, ye know. Well, not ezactly a baby, nuther, but er little gal like. Le's see, she air sevingteen now; well, she wer 'bout five er six, er sich a matter, then. Mebbe she mought know ye too."

D'Antinac, as he listened to this, began to understand that in some way he had been identified in the old man's mind as a long-lost son, and it seemed to him that his only safety lay in ready and pliant acceptance, if not in active furtherance, of the illusion. He was roughly hustled into the Hodson dwelling, a squat old house, built of pine logs, with the cracks between boarded over with clapboards.

"Sarah, der ye 'member this yer little rooster?" Hodson exclaimed, with a ring of pride in his stubborn voice, as he twisted D'Antinac around so as to bring him face to face with a slim, sallow, wrinkled little old woman, who stood by an enormous fireplace, smoking an oily-looking clay pipe. "Don't he jest hev a sort er nat'ral look ter ye? Hev he be'n killed in the wa', Sarah, eh?"

The woman did not respond immediately. She took the pipe from her mouth and gazed at D'Antinac. Her face slowly assumed a yearning look, and at length, with a sort of moaning cry of recognition, she fell upon him and clasped him close, kissing him and wetting him with her tears. Her breath, heavy with the malodor of nicotine, almost strangled him, but he dared not resist.

During this ordeal he got broken glimpses of a bright girlish face, a heavy rimpled mass of lemon-colored hair, and a very pretty form clothed in a loose home-spun gown.

"Mandy, hit air Dave come back, yer brother Dave; do yer 'member 'im?" he heard the old man say. "Do yer 'member the little rooster 'at they conscripted an' tuck erway ter the wa'? Well, thet air's him, thet air's Dave! Go kiss 'im, Mandy."

The girl did not move, nor did she seem at all inclined to share the excitement of her parents.

"Go kiss yer bud, Mandy, I say," Hodson commanded. "He wus n't killed in no wa'. Kiss the little rooster, Mandy."

"Won't," stubbornly responded Mandy.

"Well, now, I'll jest ber dinged, sis, ef this yere hain't jest too bad," the old man exclaimed in a whining, deprecatory tone of voice, quite different from the gruff, bullying sounds usually emitted by him. "I would n't er thort 'at ye'd 'fuse ter be glad w'en yer little brother come."

" 'Tain't none o' my brother, neither," she said, blushing vermilion, as she half shyly gazed at D'Antinac, with her finger in her mouth.

Mrs. Hodson hung upon the young man for a space that seemed to him next to interminable, and when at last she unwound her bony arms from his neck and pushed him back, so as to get a good look at him, he felt such relief as comes with the first fresh breath after a season of suffocation.

" Ye air be'n gittin' rich, hain't ye, Dave? an' ye air fatter 'n ye wus, too," she remarked. Then she went back to the hearth and relighted her pipe, meantime eyeing him curiously.

D'Antinac never before had found himself so utterly at a loss for something to do or say. The occasion was a singularly dry, queer, and depressing one. He felt the meanness of his attitude, and yet a side glance at Hodson's stubbornly cruel face and giant form was enough to enforce its continuance.

"Yer mammy's jest as purty es ever, *hain't* she, Dave?" said the old man with a wheedling note in his rasping voice; "she hain't changed none, *hev* she, Dave?"

"I don't know — I guess — well, perhaps she's more flesh — that is, stouter than when — than when" —

"Ye-e-s, that air hit, Dave," said Hodson, "she air fatter."

Nothing could have been more ridiculous than this assertion. Mrs. Hodson, like most old mountain women who live on salt pork and smoke tobacco, was as thin and dried up as a last year's beech-leaf. D'Antinac sheepishly glanced at Mandy. The girl put her hand over her really sweet-looking mouth and uttered a suppressed titter, at the same time deepening her blushes and shrugging her plump, shapely shoulders.

"Well, Dave, jest es I 'spected, Mandy hev furgot ye," said Hodson; "but ye know she wer' not no bigger 'n a nubbin o' dry

weather co'n w'en ye wer' tuck away. But
hit's all right, Dave; yer mammy an' me
hev allus felt like ye 'd turn up some day,
an' lo an' behole, ye hev."

Once more D'Antinac bravely tried to
deny this alleged kinship to the Hodson
household, but the old man instantly flew
into a passion and threatened all sorts of
condign punishment, not the worst of
which was "swiping him all over a' acre
o' groun'."

"But, my dear sir, I can't afford to have
you for a moment think" —

"Dry up, ye little sniv'lin' conscript, er
I'll mop this yere floo' wi' ye in a minute!
Hain't ye got no sense 't all? Hev I got
ter down ye ag'in?"

D'Antinac could not help himself. He
made a full surrender, and accepted, for
the time, his rôle of returned son and brother, trusting that something would soon
turn up to free him from the embarrass-
ment. He was not long in discovering

that Mrs. Hodson's faith in his identity was much weaker than the old man's, and as for Mandy, she very flatly refused to accept him as a brother.

It was now sundown, and the evening shadows were gathering in the valley. Far and near, the brown thrushes, the cardinal grosbeaks, and the catbirds were singing in the hedges of sassafras that overgrew the old worm fences of the Hodson farm. The woods along the mountain-sides were almost black with their heavy leafage, and the stony peaks of the highest ridge in the west, catching the reflection from the sunset clouds, looked like heaps of gold. A peculiar dryness seemed to pervade earth, air, and sky, as if some underground volcanic heat had banished every trace of moisture from the soil, whilst the sun had desiccated the atmosphere. Even the clouds, scudding overhead, had the look of being crisp and withered.

With all a Sand Mountain man's faith in

the universal efficacy of fried bacon, Hodson ordered supper to be prepared. Mandy
rolled up the sleeves of her homespun
dress, showing arms as white and plump
as those of a babe, and proceeded to cut
some long slices of streaked " side-meat," as
the mountaineers term smoked breakfast-
bacon, while her father started a fire on
the liberal hearth.   The supper was rather
greasy, but not unpalatable, the fried corn-
bread and crisp meat being supplemented
by excellent coffee. During the meal
Hodson plied D'Antinac with questions as
to where he had spent all these years of
absence, questions very hard to answer satisfactorily.

Mrs. Hodson silently watched the young
man, with a doubting, wistful look in her
watery eyes, as if she could not make up
her mind to trust him wholly, and yet
was anxious to accept him as her long-lost
son. Mandy scarcely lifted her face after
she sat down at the table, but D'Antinac

fancied he could detect a dimpling ripple of suppressed merriment about her rosy cheeks and mouth.

When supper was over, and Mandy had washed the dishes and put them away, Hodson proposed music; he was almost hilarious.

"Ye ricollec' Jord, don't ye, Dave? Our ole nigger feller—course ye do, yer boun' ter ricollec' 'im, could n't never furgit 'im; mean ole villyun, but er good hand ter hoe cotting an' pull fodder. Well, he 's jest got in from the upper co'n-fiel', an' is er feedin' 'is mule. Soon es he comes ter 'is cabing, I 'll call 'im in ter pick the banjer fur ye, an' I don't whant ye ter say nothin' 'bout who ye air, an' see ef he 'members ye."

Of course D'Antinac assented; there was nothing else for him to do. In fact, he was beginning to feel a sharp interest in the progress of this queer farce. He tried to get a look into Mandy's roguish eyes, that he might be sure of her sympathy; but she avoided him, her cheeks all the time burning with blushes, and her yellowish hair tossed loosely over her neck and shoulders. Presently Hodson went out to bring in Jord and the banjo. It was during his absence, and while Mrs. Hodson was stooping over the embers on the hearth, trying to scoop up a coal to light her pipe, that the bashful girl got up and walked across the room. As she passed D'Antinac, she whispered: —

"Ye must 'member Jord soon es ye see 'im — don't ye fail. Save er rumpus."

"All right," whispered D'Antinac.

Hodson reëntered in due time, followed by a slender, bony negro man, whose iron-gray wool and wrinkled face indexed his age at near seventy years.

"Jording, der ye know this yere gentleman?" said Hodson, pointing at D'Antinac and grinning triumphantly.

"Naw, sah, don't fink er do," answered

the negro, twirling his banjo in a self-conscious way, and bowing obsequiously.

Mrs. Hodson and Mandy interchanged half-frightened grimaces, followed by furtive glances toward the man of the house.

" Jording," said Hodson, " ef ye don't tell me who this yere feller air in less 'n a minute, I 'll jest nat'rally take the ramrod out'n Hornet," pointing to a long rifle that hung over the door, " an' I 'll jest wax hit to ye, tell ye 'll be glad ter 'member mos' anybody.   Now talk it out quick ! "

Mandy gave D'Antinac a sign with her eyes. Mrs. Hodson clasped her thin, work-worn hands.

" Why, Jord, old fellow, don't you remember Dave ! " exclaimed D'Antinac, taking a step forward, and simulating great joy and surprise.

" W-w-w'at Dave is yer tarkin' 'bout ? " stammered the poor old negro.

Hodson's face instantly swelled with rage, and he certainly would have done

"W—W—W'AT DAVE IS YER TARKIN' 'BOUT?"

something desperate had not D'Antinac just then closed up the space between himself and Jord. Mandy, too, joined the group and whispered: —

"Don't be er fool, Jord, say hit's Dave come back f'om the wa'."

Jord's wits and conscience were a little refractory, but Mandy's voice found an able auxiliary in the fact that Hodson had by this time got possession of the rifle-ramrod, and was flourishing it furiously.

"W'y, Mars Dave! dis you? 'Clar' ter goodness de ole niggah's eyes gittin' pow'-ful pore! Did n' know yer no mo'n nuffin' at fus'; but yer look jes' es nat'ral es der ole mule ter me now. Wha' ye been all dis time, Mars Dave? 'Clar' ter goodness ye 'sprise de ole niggah's senses mos' out'n 'im, yer does fo' sho'!"

While Jord was thus delivering himself, he kept one eye queerly leering at D'Antinac, and the other glaring wildly at the wavering ramrod.

" Ther', what 'd I tell ye ? " exclaimed Hodson vociferously; " what 'd I tell ye ! Jord 'members 'im ! Hit *air* Dave, sho 's ye bo'n, Sarah ! Hit air our boy, fur a fac', the blamed little rooster ! He wus n't killed in no wa', Sarah ! I allus tole ye 'at he 'd come back, an' sho' 'nuff, yer he air ! Hallooyer ! " As he spoke he capered awkwardly over the floor to the imminent danger of every one's toes. When his ecstasy had somewhat abated, he turned to Jord, his face beaming with delight.

" Now, Jording," he said, " give us my favoryte song; an', Jording, put on the power, put on the power ! This yere 's a 'cashun of onlimited rejoicin' ! Hain't it, Sarah ? "

" Hit air," responded Mrs. Hodson, puffing lazily at her old pipe.

Hodson took a chair, placed it close beside his wife, sat down with his hand caressing her shoulder, and whispered : —

" Hain't this yere jest glor'ous ? "

" Hit air," she answered lifelessly.

Mandy's face was as pink as the petals of a wild rose, and her heart was fluttering strangely.

D'Antinac, keenly alive to the dramatic situation, and somewhat troubled as to how it was to end, glanced around the room, and, despite his mental perturbation, became aware of the rude but powerful setting of the scene. The pine-smoked walls and ceiling, the scant, primitive furniture, the scrupulously clean puncheon floor, the long flint-locked rifle, the huge "stick and dirt" fireplace, the broad, roughly laid hearth, and the smoke-grimed wooden crane, all taken together, made an *entourage* in perfect accord with the figures, the costumes, and the predicament.

Jord tuned his banjo with some show of faltering, and presently he began to play and sing. The following, which were the closing stanzas, will serve to give an idea of the performance: —

" Ab'um Linkum say he gwine ter
Free ole niggah in de wah,
But Mars Hodson say he mine ter
See how Ab'um do dat dar !
  Hoop-te-loody, how ye gwine ter
  When Mars Hodson not er mine ter ?

" Den ole Ab'um say : 'You free um ! '
But Mars Hodson cut an' shoot,
An' say to Ab'um dat he see 'um
At de debbil 'fore he do 't !
  Hoop-te-loody, how ye gwine ter
  When Mars Hodson not er mine ter ? "

" That air a fac'," exclaimed Hodson almost gleefully, " that air a fac'. Here 's what never guv in yit, Dave ! They tried fur ter mek me fight fur the Confed'ret States an' they never done hit, an' 'en they tried ter conscrip' me, like they did you, Dave, but I cut 'em an' shot 'em an' hid out aroun' in these yere woods tell they guv my place the name o' Hide-out, an' they did n't conscrip' me, nuther ; an' 'en the tother gov'ment proclamated an' sot ever'body's niggers free, but yer daddy hel' on ter his one lone nigger jes' ter show 'em 'at he could, fur ther 's not a gov'ment onto the top side o' yearth 'at kin coerce er subjugate yer daddy, Dave."

Jord hung his head in the utmost humility while his master was speaking. A keen pang of sympathy shot through D'Antinac's bosom. The thought that this kindly-faced old negro was still a slave, the one lone man of his race, whose shackles remained unbroken, was touching beyond compare. And yet it seemed in consonance with the nature of things that such a person as Hodson should be able, situated as he was, to resist, for any length of time, the tide of the new régime. This easy turn from the absurd to the pathetic gave a new force to the situation, hardening and narrowing its setting, whilst it added infinite depth to its meaning. Here indeed, was the very heart of Sand Mountain, and well might it be called Hodson's Hide-out, where slavery's last victim had been hidden safe from the broad eyes of freedom.

D'Antinac could not sleep when at last he had been left by Hodson in a little dingy room, whither his gun and pack had also been transported. The bed was soft and clean, and the moonlight pouring through a low, square, paneless window invited to sleep; he lay there pondering and restless. Hodson's last words, before bidding him good-night, kept ringing in his ears : —

" Thet ole Jording air a livin' ezample o' my 'termination an' ondurence, Dave, an' hit shows what stuff yer daddy 's made out'n. The whole etarnal worl' kin never free that air nigger. He er mine ter keep, es the ole hymn say, 'whatever may erpose.' "

D'Antinac was small of stature and not at all a hero mentally; but he had come of a liberty loving ancestry, and was, despite his foreign looking name, an American to his heart's core. No doubt the wild roving life he had for years been leading, as an emissary of an ornithological society, had served to emphasize and accentuate his love of freedom in every sense.

He had turned and tossed on his bed for several hours, when a peculiar voice, between a chant and a prayer in its intonations, came in through the little window, along with the white stream of moonlight. He got up and softly went to the aperture. The voice came from a little detached cabin in the back yard. It was Jord praying.

"Lor', hab de ole man sarb ye well an' true? Mus' I die er slabe an' come 'ome ter glory wid de chain on? What I done, Lor', 'at ye 'zart me when I 'se ole? Is I nebber gwine ter be free? Come down, Lor', an', 'stain de ole man in he 'fliction an' trouble, an', O Lor', gib 'im ole eyes one leetle glimp' ob freedom afore he die. Amen."

Such were the closing words of the plaintive and touching prayer. No wonder that suddenly D'Antinac's whole life focused itself in the desire to liberate that old slave. He forgot every element of his predicament, save his nearness to the last remnant of human bondage. He drew on his clothes, seized his pack and gun, and slyly crept out through the little window. The cool, sweet mountain air braced him like wine. This ought to be the breath of freedom. These rugged peaks surrounding the little " pocket " or valley ought not to fence in a slave or harbor a master.

Riley Hodson slept soundly all night, and did not get up before breakfast was ready.

" Let the little rooster sleep ; hit air Sunday, anyhow ; let 'im git up when he whants ter," said the old man, when D'Antinac failed to appear.

Mandy had fried some ham and eggs for breakfast, and she came to the table clad in a very becoming calico gown. Mrs. Hodson appeared listless, and her eyes had no cheerful light in them. The old man ate ravenously the choicest eggs and the best slices of ham, with the air of one determined upon vicariously breaking the fast of the entire household. But Mandy had saved back in the frying-pan some extra bits for the young stranger.

An hour passed.

" Guess the blamed little rooster air a-goin' ter snooze all day. Mebbe I 'd better wake 'im," Hodson at last said, and went to the little bedroom. He tapped on the door, but got no response. Then he pounded heavily and called out : —

" Hullo, Dave ! "

Silence followed. He turned and glared at Mrs. Hodson, then at Mandy.

" The blamed little rooster ! " he muttered, flinging open the door. For many seconds he stood peering into the room. Presently he clutched the doorpost to steady himself, then he reeled round, and his face grew white.

" Dave er gone ! " he gasped ; " Dave er gone ! Lor-r-d, Sarah, he air gone ag'in ! "

Almost involuntarily Mandy went to the bedroom door and confirmed her father's assertion.   Mrs. Hodson was quiet. Indeed, there seemed to have fallen a perfect hush over the valley and the mountains.

Riley Hodson soon rallied.   He sprang to his feet like a tiger.

" Mandy," he stormed, " go tell Jording ter bridle an' saddle the mule, quick ! "

Mandy went at his command, as if blown by his breath.   In a few minutes she returned, white as a ghost, and gasped : —

" Jord er gone ! "

" What !   How !   Gone !   Jording ! "

" He air gone," Mandy repeated, holding out a two-dollar " greenback " bill in one hand and a piece of writing-paper in the other.

" I got these yere off 'n Jord's table."

With great difficulty and in a breathless way, she read aloud what was hastily scrawled on the paper : —

Mr. Hodson :

Dear Sir, — You are greatly mistaken; I am not your son. I never saw you or any member of your family in my life before yesterday. Your wife and daughter are both well aware of your curious illusion. Jordan, whom I take with me to freedom, knows that I am not your lost son. In fact, I am,

Very respectfully yours,
David D'Antinac.

P. S.   A letter will reach me if directed in care of the Smithsonian Institution at Washington, D. C.   I inclose two dollars to pay for the trouble I have given you.

Hodson caught his mule, bridled it and

saddled it, and rode away up the zigzag mountain trail in pursuit of the fugitives; but he did not catch them. At nightfall he returned in a sombre mood, with a look of dry despair in his eyes. For a long while he did not speak; but at length, when his wife came and sat down close beside him, he muttered : —

"Wer' hit Dave, Sarah ? "

"Hit wer' not," she answered; "Dave never had no mole onter 'is chin."

RUDGIS AND GRIM

" When Freedom from her mountain height."

THE Rudgis farm was the only one in
Lone Ridge Pocket, a secluded nook of
the North Georgia mountain-region, and its
owner, Eli Rudgis, was, in the ante-bellum
time, a man among the simple and honest
people who dwelt beside the little crooked
highway leading down the valley of the
Pine-log Creek. He owned but one negro, as was often the case with them, and
he had neither wife nor children. His
slave was his sole companion of the human kind, sharing with certain dogs, pigs,
horses, and oxen a rude, democratic dis-
tribution of favors and frowns. As a man
this negro was an interesting specimen of
the genuine African: short, strongly built,
but ill-shapen, with a large head firmly

braced by a thick, muscular neck on broad, stooping shoulders; a skin as black as night; small deep-set eyes; a protruding, resolute jaw; and a nose as flat as the head of an adder. As a slave he was, perhaps, valuable enough in his way; but both as man and thrall he did no discredit to his name, which was Grim. He, too, was a familiar figure along the Pine-log road, as he drove an old creaking ox-cart to and from the village.

When the war broke out, master and slave had reached the beginning of the downward slope of life, and, having spent many years together in their lonely retreat at the Pocket, had grown to love each other after the surly, taciturn fashion of men who have few thoughts and a meagre gift of expression.

Eli Rudgis was tall, slim, cadaverous, slow of movement, and sallow; but he had a will of his own, and plenty of muscle to enforce it withal.

GRIM

" Grim," said he one day, " them derned Northerners air a-goin' ter set ye free."

The negro looked up from the hickory-bark basket he was mending, and scowled savagely at his master.

" W'at yo' say, Mars' Rudgis?" he presently inquired.

" Them Yankees air a-goin' ter gi' ye yer freedom poorty soon."

Grim's face took on an expression of dogged determination, his shoulders rose almost to the level of his protruding ears, and his small, wolfish eyes gleamed fiercely.

" Who say dey gwine ter do dat?" he demanded with slow, emphatic enunciation.

" I say hit, an' w'en I says hit," began the master; but Grim broke in with : —

" Dey cayn't do nuffin' wid me. I done made up my mine; dis chil' cayn't be fo'ced. Yo' yah dat, Mars' Rudgis?"

Rudgis grinned dryly, and walked away, smoking his cob-pipe with the air of a philosopher who bides his time.

The Rudgis cabin was a low, nonde-
script log structure of three or four rooms
and a wide entry or hall, set in the midst of
a thick, luxuriant orchard of peach, plum,
and apple trees crowning a small conical
foothill, which, seen from a little distance,
appeared to rest against the rocky breast
of the mountain that stood over against
the mouth of the Pocket. From the rickety veranda, where Rudgis now sought a
seat, there was a fine view of the little
farm, whose angular but rolling patches of
tillable land straggled away to the foothills
on the other side of the Pocket, beyond
which the wall of cliffs rose, gray and
brown, to a great height.

Recently Eli Rudgis had been thinking
a good deal about Grim; for, as the war
continued, it grew in his mind that the
South was going to lose the fight. He
had only recently heard of President Lin-
coln's emancipation proclamation, and with
that far-seeing prudence characteristic of

a certain order of provincial intellect he was considering how best to forestall the effect of freedom if it should come, as he feared it would. Grim was his property, valued at about eight hundred dollars in "good money," or in Confederate scrip at perhaps two or three thousand dollars, more or less. He shrank from selling the negro, for in his dry, peculiar way he was fond of him ; but, on the other hand, he could not consent to lose so much money on the outcome of an issue not of his own making. It can readily be imagined how, with ample leisure for reflection, and with no other problem to share his attention, Rudgis gradually buried himself, so to speak, in this desire to circumvent and nullify emancipation (in so far as it would affect his ownership of Grim) when it should come.

Grim was far more knowing, far better informed, and much more of a philosopher, than his master gave him credit for being.

By some means, as occult as reliable, he had kept perfectly abreast of the progress of the great weltering, thundering, death-dealing tempest of the war, and in his heart he felt the coming of deliverance, the jubilee of eternal freedom for his race. Incapable, perhaps, of seeing clearly the true aspect of what was probably in store for him, he yet experienced a change of prospect that affected every fibre of his imagination, and opened wide every pore of his sensibility. Naturally wary, suspicious, and quick to observe signs, he had been aware that his master was revolving some scheme, which in all probability would affect a change in their domestic relations, to the extent, possibly, of severing the tie which for so long had bound together the lord and the thrall of Lone Ridge Pocket.

"He studyin' 'bout er-sellin' me," he soliloquized, as he lingered over his task of basket-mending after Rudgis had gone, "an' he fink he er-gwine ter fool dis ol' coon. Well, 'fore de Lor', mebbe he will."

" What ye mutterin' thar, Grim ? " called the master from his seat on the veranda. " What ye growlin' 'bout, lak er pup over er ham-bone ? "

" Nuffin', sah ; I jes' tryin' fo' ter ketch dat chune w'at I be'n er-l'arnin'."

Then to clench the false statement, Grim began humming :—

> " De coon he hab er eejit wife,
>   Hoe yo' co'n, honey,
>   De coon he hab er eejit wife,
>   An' she nebber comb her hah in 'er life,
>   Keep er-hoein' yo' co'n, honey.

> " An' de coon say : ' I knows w'at I 'll do,'
>   Hoe yo' co'n, honey,
>   An' his wife she squall out, ' I does too ! '
>   An' she snatch 'im poorty nigh in two,
>   Keep er-hoein' yo' co'n, honey.

> " So dat coon he allus ricollec',
>   Hoe yo' co'n, honey,
>   Ef he talk too loud he mus' expec'
>   She scratch he eyes an' wring he neck,
>   Keep er-hoein' yo' co'n, honey ! "

Rudgis listened stoically enough, so far as facial expression went; but when the low, softly melodious song was done, he shook his head, and smiled aridly.

"Got more sense 'an er Philadelphy laryer," he muttered under his breath, "an' he's got some undertakin' inter that noggin er his'n. S'pect I hev ter do somethin' er nother wi' him, er he's er-goin' ter git the best o' me."

He drew away at his wheezing pipe, leaning his chin, thinly fringed with grizzled beard, in his left hand, and propping that arm with his knee. His typical mountain face wore a puzzled, half-worried, half-amused expression.

"Dern 'is black pictur'," he continued inaudibly, though his lips moved; "he air a-considerin' freedom right now."

> "Whi' man tuk me fer er fool,
>   Hoe yo' co'n, honey,
> Wo'k me like er yaller mule,
> An' never gi' me time ter cool,
>   Keep er-hoein' yo' co'n, honey,"

hummed Grim in that tender falsetto of his. There was a haze in the air, a May-time shimmer over the Pocket and up the terraced slopes of the mountains. Suddenly a heavy booming, like distant thunder, tumbled as if in long, throbbing waves across the peaks, and fell into the little drowsy cove.

" W'at dat, Mars' Rudgis? 'Fore de Lor', w'at dat?" cried the negro, leaping to his feet, and staring stupidly, his great mouth open, his long arms akimbo.

Eli Rudgis took his pipe-stem from his mouth, and sat in a harkening attitude. " Hit's thet air war er-comin'," he presently said, and resumed his smoking and reflections.

" De good Lor', Mars' Rudgis, w'at we gwine ter do?" stammered Grim, his heavy countenance growing strangely ashen over its corrugated blackness.

" Shet erp, an' mend that ther' basket," growled the master. " Goin' ter mek ye

wo'k like the devil er-beatin' tan-bark while
I kin: fer thet's yer frien's er-comin', ter
free ye, Grim, shore 's shootin'."

The African bowed his head over his
light task, and remained thoughtfully silent, while the dull pounding in the far
distance increased to an incessant roar,
vague, wavering, suggestive, awful.

Rudgis thought little of the wider significance accompanying that slowly rolling
tempest of destruction ; his mental vision
was narrowed to the compass of the one
subject which lately had demanded all his
powers of consideration. Was it possible
for him to hold Grim as his slave despite
the Proclamation of Emancipation, and
notwithstanding the triumph of the Federal
armies ?

" Ef I try ter take 'im down the country
ter sell 'im, they 'll conscrip' me inter the
war," he argued to himself, " an' ef I stays
yer them 'fernal Yankees 'll set 'im free.
Seem lak it air pow'ful close rubbin' an',

dern ef I know what ter do! I air kind
o' twixt the skillet an' the coals."

Day after day he sat smoking and cogi-
tating, while Grim pottered at this or that
bit of labor. He had an unconquerable
aversion to going into the army, a thing
he had avoided, partly by reason of his
age and partly by one personal shift or another, after the exigencies of the Confeder-
acy had led to the conscription of "able-
bodied men" regardless of age. He felt
that things were growing to desperate
straits in the low country, and he feared to
show himself outside his mountain fastness
lest a conscript officer might nab him and
send him to the front. Not that he was a
coward; but in the high, dry atmosphere
of the hill country there lingered a sweet
and inextinguishable sense of loyalty to
the old flag, which touched the minds of
many mountaineers with a vague intimation of the enormity of rebellion against the
government of Washington and Jackson.

And yet they were Southerners, good fighters, Yankee-haters, and clung to the right of property in their negroes with a tenacity as tough as the sinews of their hardy limbs. They were, indeed, far more stubborn in this last regard than any of the great slave-owners of the low country, owing, no doubt, to their narrow, provincial notions of personal independence, which felt no need for aid, or for the interference of the law in their private concerns.

Grim was not a typical slave, but he was a legitimate instance of the slavery known in the secluded region of the Southern mountain country. He was as free, in all but name, as were most illiterate laborers of that day, barring that his skin and the Southern traditions set him on a plane far below and quite detached from that of the lowest white men. He had no bonds that galled him personally; plenty to eat, just enough work to keep him robust, a

good bed, sufficient clothing, and unlimited
tobacco — what more could he want?

His master, however, observed that he
was doing a great deal of thinking; that
lately he was busying his mind with some
absorbing problem, and from certain signs
and indications the fact appeared plain
that Grim was making ready to meet the
day of freedom. Rudgis saw this with a
dull, deep-seated sentimental pang mixed
with anger and resentment. Years of
companionship in that lonely place had
engendered a fondness for his slave of
which he was not fully aware, and out of
which was now issuing a sort of bewilder-
ment of mind and soul. Would Grim indeed forsake him, desert him to go away
to try the doubtful chances of a new order
of things? This question was supplemented by another on a different stratum
of human selfishness. Rudgis like all
mountain-men, had a narrow eye to profit
and loss. The money represented by

Grim as his slave possessed a powerful influence; it was the larger part of his fortune.

Grim, on his part, watched his master as the tide of war flowed on through the mountain-gaps far to the west of the Pocket; his calculations were simpler and more directly personal than those of his master. Of course things could not remain in this situation very long. Grim was the first to speak straight to the subject.

"Mars' Rudgis," said he one day, "yo' be'n 'siderin' erbout sellin' me."

This direct accusation took the master unawares.

"Wha-wha-what 's that air ye air er-sayin', ye ol' whelp?" he spluttered, almost dropping his pipe.

"Yo' be'n er-finkin' 'at I 's gittin' close onter de freedom line, an' ye s'pose yo' 'd better git w'at ye kin fo' me, yah-yah-yah-ee-oorp!" and the black rascal broke forth with a mighty guffaw, bending himself almost double, and slapping his hands vigorously. "But yo''s feared dey git ye an' mek yo' tote er gun, an' 'at yo''d git de stuffin' shot outen yo' ef yo' try take me down de country, yah-yah-yah-ee-ee-oorp!"

"Shet erp! What ye mean? Stop thet air sq'allin', er I 'll " —

"Yah-yah-yah-ee-eep! I done cotch onter yo' ca'c'lation, Mars' Rudgis, 'fo' de Lor' I has, oh! Yah-yah-yah-yah-ha-eep! An' yo' fink I 's er eejit all dis time, yah-yah-yah! Oh, gi' 'long, Mars' Rudgis, yo' cayn't fool dis chicken, yah-ha-yah-ha-ha-ha-ee-eer-pooh!"

Rudgis tried several times to stop this flow of accusative mirth, but at last, quite confused, he stood tall and gaunt, with a sheepish grin on his dry, wrinkled face, gazing at the writhing negro as he almost screamed out his sententious but fluent revelation.

"I done be'n er-watchin' yo' like er

sparrer-hawk watchin' er peewee, Mars' Rudgis, an' I say ter myself: 'Jes' see 'im er-figerin' how much I 's wo'f, an' how much he gwine ter lose w'en I goes free. An' I done be'n jes' er-bustin' over it all dis time, yah-yah-yah-ee-ee!'"

"Grim," said Rudgis, presently, with slow, emphatic expression, "I air er-goin' 'mejitly ter give ye one whirpin' 'at ye 'll ricomember es long es they 's breath in yer scurvy ol' body!"

They were standing on the veranda at the time. Rudgis turned into the entry, and immediately came out with a ramrod in his hand.

"Now fer yer sass ye air er-goin' ter ketch hit," he said, in that cold, rasping tone which means so much. "Stan' erp yer an' take yer med'cine."

Grim went down on his knees and began to beg; his mirth had vanished; he was trembling violently. Rudgis had never whipped him.

" Fo' de Lor' sake, Mars' Eli, don' w'irp
de po' ol' chil'! I war jes funnin', Mars'
Rudgis; I jes' want ter see w'at yo' gwine
say. I "—

At that moment there was a great clat-
ter of iron-shod hoofs at the little yard
gate; the next, three or four horses
bounded over the low fence and dashed up
to the veranda.

" Please, Mars' Rudgis, don' w'irp me! I
did n' mean no harm, Mars' Rudgis,' deed
I did n'! Oh, fo' de Lor' sake!"

" Ha! there! stop that!" commanded a
loud, positive voice. "What the devil do
you mean!"

Rudgis had already looked that way.
He saw some mounted soldiers, wearing
blue uniforms and bearing bright guns,
glaring at him.

" Oh, Mars' Rudgis, I never gwine do so
no mo', don' w'irp me! don' w'irp me!"
continued Grim, paying no heed to the
soldiers.

"Le' me off dis yer time, fo' de goo' Lor' sake!" And he held up his hands in dramatic beseechment.

"If you strike that negro one blow, I 'll shoot a hole through you quicker than lightning!" roared one of the men, who appeared to be an officer, at the same time leveling his pistol.

Rudgis dropped the ramrod as if he had been suddenly paralyzed. Grim sprang to his feet with the agility of a black cat.

"What does this mean?" demanded the officer, showing a gleam of anger in his eyes, his voice indicating no parleying mood.

Rudgis stood there, pale, stolid, silent, his mouth open, his arms akimbo.

"Lor', sah, we jes' er-foolin'," said Grim, seeing that his master could find not a word to say. "We 's er-playin' hoky-poky."

The officer leaned over his saddle-bow, and looked from one to the other of the culprits.

" Yes, sah it war bony-hokus 'at we 's er-playin', 'zac'ly dat, sah," continued Grim.

" Playing what ? " grimly inquired the officer.

" Rokus-pokus, sah."

" You lying old scamp," cried the officer, glaring at him, " you 're trying to deceive me ! "

" Ax Mars' Rudgis, now ; ax him, sah."

" Humph ! " and the Federal officer turned to the master. " What do you say, sir ? "

" Tell 'im, Mars' Rudgis ; 'bout w'at we 's er-playin'," pleaded Grim.

Rudgis moved his lips as if to speak, but they were dry and made no sound. He licked them with his furred, feverish tongue. Never before had he been so thoroughly frightened.

" Are you dumb ? " stormed the officer, again handling his weapon. " Can't you speak ? "

" Hit were hoky-poky," gasped Rudgis.

"Dah, now! Dah, now! Mebbe yo's sat'sfied, sah. W'a''d I tol' yo'?" cried Grim, wagging his head and gesticulating. "We's jes' er-playin' dat leetle game."

The officer wanted some information about a road over the mountain, so he made Grim saddle a mule and go with him to show the way. As he rode off he called back to Rudgis: —

"This man's as free as you are, and he need n't come back if he don't want to."

When they were quite gone, and the last sound of their horses' feet had died away down in the straggling fringe of trees at the foot of the hill, Rudgis picked up his ramrod and looked at it quizzically, as if he expected it to speak. Slowly his face relaxed, and a queer smile drew it into leathery wrinkles.

"Hit were hoky-poky, by gum!" he muttered. "The dern ol' scamp!"

Presently he filled his pipe, and lighted it, grinning all the while, and saying: —

HE FILLED HIS PIPE, AND LIGHTED IT

" The triflin' ol' rooster, he hed half er
dozen dif'ent names fer it; but hit were
hoky-poky jes' the same. The dern old
coon!"

The day passed, likewise the night;
but Grim did not return. A week, a
month, six months; no Grim, no mule.
Sherman had swept through Georgia, and
on up through the Carolinas; Johnston
and Lee had surrendered. Peace had
fallen like a vast silence after the awful din
of war. The worn and weary soldiers of
the South were straggling back to their
long-neglected homes to resume as best
they could the broken threads of their
peaceful lives.

Rudgis missed Grim more as a companion than as a slave. He mourned for him,
in a way, recalling his peculiarities, and
musing over that one superb stroke of wit
by which, perhaps, his life had been saved.
Never did he fail, at the end of such rev-
erie, to repeat, more sadly and tenderly

each time, " Hit *war* hoky - poky, blame his ol' hide ! " The humor of this verbal reference was invariably indicated by a peculiar rising inflection in pronouncing " were," by which he meant to accentuate lovingly Grim's prompt prevarication.

Spring had come again to the mountains, bringing its gush of greenery, its mellow sunshine, and its riotous birds. Into the Pocket blew a breeze, soft, fragrant, dream - burdened, eddying like a river of sweets around the lonely, embowered cabin.

Early one morning Rudgis was smoking in his accustomed seat on the veranda. In his shirt-sleeves, bareheaded and barefooted, his cotton shirt open wide at throat and bosom, he looked like a bronze statue of Emancipation, so collapsed, wrinkled, and sear was he. His Roman nose was the only vigorous feature of his unkempt and retrospective face.

The sound of a mule's feet trotting up

the little stony road did not attract his
curiosity, albeit few riders passed that
way; but when Grim came suddenly in
sight, it was an apparition that relaxed
every fibre of Rudgis's frame. He dropped
lower in the old armchair, his arms fell
limp, and his mouth opened wide, letting
fall the cob-pipe. He stared helplessly.

"Yah I is, Mars' Rudgis; got back at
las'. How ye do, Mars' Rudgis?"

There was a ring of genuine delight in
the negro's voice, — the *timbre* of loyal
sentiment too sweet for expression in written language. He slid from the mule's
back, — not the same mule that he had
ridden away, but an older and poorer one,
— and scrambled through the lopsided
gate.

"Well, by dad!" was all Rudgis could
say; "well, by dad!" His lower jaw wab-
bled and sagged.

"Tol' yo' dey could n't sot dis niggah
free, did n' I?" cried Grim, as he made

a dive for both his old master's hands.
" I 's come back ter 'long ter yo' same lak
I allus did.   Yah, sah ; yah, sah."

Rudgis arose slowly from his seat and
straightened up his long, lean form so
that he towered above the short, sturdy
negro.   He looked down at him in silence
for some moments, his face twitching
strangely.   Slowly the old-time expression
began to appear around his mouth and
eyes.   With a quick step he went into the
house, and returned almost instantly, bearing a ramrod in his hand.

"Well, Grim," he said, with peculiar
emphasis, "ef ye air still my prop'ty, an'
ye don't objec', s'posin' we jes' finish up
that air leetle game er hoky-poky what we
was er playin' w'en them Yankees kem
an' bothered us."

A RACE ROMANCE

For many years Wiley Brimson had been the owner of Sassafras Pocket, a small but fertile nook between two great projections of what is known as the Pine-log Mountain in Cherokee, Georgia. He owned one slave, a coal-black negro, whom for the greater part of his lifetime he had threatened with condign freedom.

"Ef they air anythin' 'at air pine-blank wrong," he was fond of saying, "hit air human slavery. Ther' 's thet nigger o' mine, thet nigger Rory; he 's jes' as good as I air. He hev jes' as much right ter boss me as I hev ter boss him. He orter be free; but then I cayn't stan' the expense o' settin' 'im free, fer he 's wo'th nigh onto thirteen hundred dollars. Hit air too much money ter lose."

A great deal of talk in this strain made Brimson unpopular long before the war broke out. The fact is, he was not of a disposition to be a common favorite at best, especially among the mountaineers, who are the most conservative and least argumentative folk in the world, while at the same time they are the most tenacious of their opinions, right or wrong.

Rory, the negro, was younger than his master, and had been bought by him at sheriff's sale as the legal victim sacrificed to pay the debt of a drunkard.

"Ye may thank yer lucky stars, Rory, thet I hed thet money on han' an' bought ye," Brimson often said to his slave; "fer ef I hed n't 'a' done it ye'd 'a' went down ter New Orleans jest er-callyhootin'."

This was true, for a buyer who traded in the Louisiana market was present at the sale and bid close to the margin on Rory, who at the time was a strong, fine boy of fifteen.

Brimson was a bachelor, and very naturally found Rory a most acceptable and interesting companion as well as a decidedly clever and faithful servant. The lad's droll humor and abundant animal spirits filled Sassafras Pocket with new life.

"The dern leetle rooster," said Brimson to a select company over at Peevy's still-house, — "the dern leetle rooster, he air twice as smart as two white boys. He kin sing like er tomtit, he kin climb like er squirrel; he kin run like er rabbit, an' he kin pick the banjer ekal ter er showman."

As time went by and Rory grew to stalwart manhood, his master's admiration of him confirmed itself in many ways not in the least relished by the residents of the Pine-log region.

"W'y, fellers," exclaimed Dick Redden to a group of friends, "thet ther' low-down, no-'count Brimson, he lets thet ther' nigger eat at the table with 'im, an' Gabe Holly say he see 'im bite er chaw off'n the nigger's terbacker."

"Well," remarked Dave Aikens, "I hearn 'im 'low thet he'd l'arn Rory ter read, ef he knowed how his own self."

"Gent'men," remarked Squire Lem Rookey, with a judicial reserve in his manner, "hit hev some 'pearances 'at Wiley Brimson air er dern aberlitionist."

Usually Squire Rookey's word was the final one, and from that day forth Brimson's name had attached to it the most opprobrious qualification to be found in the Southern vocabulary. The man was ostracized in the fullest sense of the word. Such friends as he had now dropped him. The meetings over at the still-house voted him out, and the children avoided passing him in the public road. He felt all this to a degree which gradually intensified his peculiarities of disposition and shut him like a hermit within the limits of Sassafras Pocket.

"Me an' my nigger kin live all ter ourselves," he growled, "an' ef folks don't jes' like our way er doin', w'y, jes' let 'em keep off'n these yer premerses."

Deprived of the social privileges and comforts hitherto grudgingly afforded him by courtesy of his wide acquaintance in Pine-log settlement, he began to thirst for education. It is not certainly known how he did get it, but in time he learned to read and write, after a fashion; and the next thing was to teach Rory, who, much to Brimson's chagrin, was anything but an apt scholar.

"He air er leetle slow an' sort o' clumsy erbout gittin' at the main p'ints o' the spellin'-book," was Brimson's self-consolation; "but then w'enever he do once git started he air er-gwine ter jest knock the socks off'n me er-l'arnin', see 'f he don't."

They usually devoted the warm part of the afternoon to the daily lessons, sitting side by side on a rude wooden bench in the shade of the vine that almost overloaded the low, wide, rickety porch on the south

side of Brimson's cabin. Through a rift
they might have a fine view of the little
valley, or pocket, beyond which the foothills swelled up, overtopped by the blue
peaks of the Pine-log range. On one hand
they had a garden and truck patch, on the
other a small area, called the plantation,
which was given over to corn and wheat
and cotton. In front, between the house
and the little gate by the roadside, was the
well with its mossy curb and long, stone-
weighted sweep. Brimson was a small
man, and as he sat by the almost giant
negro, spelling-book in hand, he looked
the very embodiment of persistent insignificance. A painter might have sketched
the twain as a study for an allegorical picture of the absorption of one race by another. The massive head and shoulders
of the negro leaned over the attenuated
white man, as if about to fall upon him
and crush him, or as if on the point of
breathing him in through the gaping,

voluptuous, and infinitely stupid mouth.
Brimson, irascibly patient and hysterically
persevering, drilled his good-natured pupil,
day in and day out, up and down the pages
of Webster's Spelling-book, and back and
forth through the mazes of McGuffey's
First Reader. To Rory all this was a
sort of fascinating and yet singularly vexa-
tious punishment, to which he went with
perfunctory promptness and from which
he escaped with a sense of taking a deep,
inspiring draught of thankfulness. He
often gazed during lesson-time on the
slender, bloodless cheeks, the sunken pale
blue eyes, and the broad, high forehead of
his master, while a vague but powerful
realization of the Caucasian's superb en-
dowments crept through his benighted
consciousness. A glimmer of ambition,
mysteriously moonlike and wan to Rory's
vision, began to spread over the much
thumbed pages of the books.

" Knowledge air power," urged Brimson

— "hit sattingly air, Rory; an' him thet reads air him thet conquers."

"Dat 's so, mars'; dat 's so," responded Rory, his voice as vacant as his face.

"Ye see," continued Brimson, crossing the attenuated index finger of his right hand over the corresponding member of his left, and drawing his earnest little face into a wisp of wrinkles — "ye see, Rory, this air er day o' liberal idees an' 'mazin' progress. Hit air the day o' fraternity an' ekal rights."

"Dat 's so, mars'; dat 's so."

"The nigger race 'll be ekal ter any race under heving jes' as soon as it kin read an' write, Rory."

"Dat 's so, mars'; dat 's so."

The years stole past, and the monotony of life in Sassafras Pocket scarcely varied a hair's breadth until the great war came on and freedom began to send its puffs of freshness and fragrance through the air in advance of the steadily moving armies of

Sherman and Grant. Rory, by some indirect flash of perception, foresaw the coming of emancipation long before his master had dared to dream of such a thing; but it brought him no special pleasure. Brimson had been fairly kind to him, and there was something in the negro's heart that drew it tenderly towards the little old man. This tenderness was neither love nor genuine respect; it was more a mere active quality of Rory's nature. In fact, between the black man and the white there had long ago risen a vague but powerful apparition of danger, which both had tried to brush aside with sentimental recognition of their need of each other.

" Hit air inlightenment thet you kin git out'n me, Rory, an' hit air work thet I kin git out'n you," argued Brimson.

" Yah, sah; dat 's so," assented Rory.

The war went crashing past them, a great roaring sea of flame and smoke and blood; but not one ripple of it found a

way into the remote security of Sassafras
Pocket. The Emancipation Proclamation
never reached them, and peace had been
established for months before they found
it out.

Meantime Brimson's patience and zealous earnestness in the cause of rescuing
Rory from heathen ignorance had risen
to higher and higher planes of self-devo-
tion; but strangely enough did the negro
respond. He developed, it is true, and
rapidly took on a most interesting veneer-
ing of knowledge, so to speak, outstripping
his teacher at certain turns of the race, and
evincing now and again a most wonderful
acumen; and yet the barbaric nature within
him seemed to deepen and broaden apace
with his educational acquirements. His
taste for baked 'possum grew more intense,
and his proficiency in banjo-picking wonderfully increased, as if his imagination
were liberating itself altogether along savage lines.

Brimson obeyed an opposite law, growing more and more pale, thin, and nervous-looking, while his hair whitened and his forehead assumed a more pronounced scholarly baldness, touched with a bland, wavering philanthropic sheen which added to his countenance, naturally none too strong, the appearance of being about to fall into a nebulous state of disintegration.

"Ye 're free now, Rory," he said one day, when at last the news had come to the pocket, "an' hit air yer juty ter show up freedom at her best paces. Look up at the flag, Rory; look up at the flag o' liberty! Hit air yer flag, Rory — yer flag thet yer forefathers fit fer at Buncombe Hill an' Sarytogy Lane! Gaze onto the yearth, Rory, fer hit jes' nat'rally berlongs ter ye. Take hit, Rory, an' rule over hit, fer ye 've yarnt hit by yer endoorin' intelligence an' patriotism!"

Rory looked up, as he was bidden, but saw no flag; and as for the earth, that part of it visible from his point of view was merely Sassafras Pocket with its rim of purple mountain-peaks.

" Hit air the leadin' doctrine o' moral ph'los'phy thet ter the victor berlongs the lands, temptations, an' haryditerments," continued Brimson, mopping his brow; " an' now air yer time er never, Rory."

"Yah, sah; dat's so, sah," said Rory. " I gwine ter 'flect on it p'intedly, sah."

The war being over and the freedom of the colored race having been accomplished, the inhabitants of the Pine-log region began slowly to relax their feelings towards Brimson, and in due time he was once more received among the visitors at the still-house, albeit he could feel that his relations with his neighbors were yet pretty violently strained, no matter what attempts were made to conceal the old dislike. He was not a man to care much for public opinion, so long as he felt that public opinion was wrong and his opinion was right;

and now that his privilege of free speech was no longer withheld, he enjoyed to the fullest airing the philosophy he had been storing during all these years of social exclusion and unremitting study.

"He air jest 'zactly the same ole aberlition eejit thet he was afore the war," exclaimed Squire Lem Rookey, whose judicial caution had been somewhat shaken by the cataclysm of rebellion, "an' I jest wush thet he hed ter maul rails under er nigger boss fer the next forty-nine years."

"I hearn Gabe Holly say thet Bud Peevy tole him thet Wiley Brimson air still er-talkin' up nigger soope'ority ter thet black Rory," remarked Sol Rowe. "Seem lak some fellers cayn't l'arn no sense w'en they hev the chaince."

The real truth was that the neighborhood viewed with surprise the turn affairs seemed to be taking over in the little pocket, where the relations between the white man and the black, although greatly altered in name, appeared to be even more profitable than under the old order of things. Brimson himself was inclined to speak boastfully of the fact that it was no loss to him that Rory had been made free.

"Look at my craps," he exclaimed; "they is bigger an' better 'an they ever was in them slavery days. Freedom an' edication hev made er enlightened laborer of Rory. He seem ter take er wider view o' the lay o' life 'an he did w'en he war in the gallin' chains of onhuman bondage."

Some of the more impatient and belli-cose men of the settlement could with diffi-culty brook Brimson's arguments and al-lusions. Personal violence surely would have been indulged in had it not been for Brimson's age and physical weakness.

"I'd slap 'im clean through onto the other side o' hisself, w'en he gits ter talkin' thet ther' way, ef he wusn't so dern puny-lookin'," remarked Bud Peevy; "but he do look more like er runt pig 'at's fed on buttermilk 'an any one man I ever see in all my life."

If there had been a disinterested on-looker at Sassafras Pocket, the proceedings there would have furnished him much food for reflection as well as no little amusement. Brimson was pressing education upon Rory with ever-increasing insistence, and the negro, though now well along in middle life, was beginning to show the first signs of genuine advance towards self-regard in the matter.

"How kin dis book-l'arnin' eber do me any good? Ain't I er nigger all de same, arter I done fill myse'f full o' dat edication?" he would demand, wagging his head half willfully, half doubtfully. "Tell me dat, now."

"W'at ef ye air er nigger? W'at do thet ermount to? Ain't the Constertootion of the Union done said 'at all men is free an' ekal? Ain't ye er man same as anybody?"

"Dat's so, boss; dat's so."

This was the first time that Rory ever had substituted " boss " for " mars'" in talking to Brimson. The latter accepted the change with all the secret pleasure of a teacher who is proud of his work.

" An' Rory, ef ye r'ally desires the rege-lar ole b'iled-down essence o' percoon-root freedom, ye mus' jest re'ch out an' take hit," he went on, as if delivering a set lec-ture to the negro, who stood before him a black giant whose massive proportions ap-peared to be increasing day by day.

" Dat's so, boss; dat's so. I's been er sorter calc'latin' 'bout dat yer lately."

" Well, I 'd s'pose hit war erbout time ye was usin' yer gumtion er leetle," continued Brimson, excited and encouraged by Rory's signs of interest. "'F I's you, I 'd take my proper position into sassiety, an' I 'd wrest f'om the white man my jus' dues. W'at hev ye done all yer life? Ye 've worked fer the white man. W'at hev ye got fer hit? Victuals an' clothes; whar 'r the land ye 've yarnt? Hit b'longs ter the white man. 'F I 's you, I 'd take hit er-way f'om 'im. Ye'r' big an' strong, ye 've got the power, an' ye'r' foolish ef ye don't use it."

" Dat 's so; dat 's so; I 's 'sturbin' my min' er mighty heap 'bout dat fing lately; sho 's you born, I is, boss."

"'Sturbin' yer mind, 'sturbin' yer mind!" cried Brimson, with eloquent impatience. "W'y don't ye act? W'y don't ye show up yer power? W'at hev I been er-larnin' ye all this time?"

Gradually, under this sort of pressure, Rory lost his childlike simplicity, and his bubbling, jocund humor was changed into something bordering on moroseness. He avoided Brimson at times and brooded aside, as if contemplating some deep and troublesome problem. Whatever it was, it took him a long while to satisfy his mind in regard to it; for the months and years went by, while he slowly changed from a careless, happy negro to a strangely reticent savage in appearance. So gradual, indeed, was this transformation, or rather *quasi* reversion to type, that Brimson did not fully realize it.

The pocket had no visitors now, the men of the Pine-log having dropped Brimson again when his doctrines of "freedom an' ekality" had become absolutely unbearable to them; and the two, the white and the black, were left undisturbed, while the former perfected the latter's education and engendered in him the full measure of a doctrine whose immense fascination at last overcame every opposition in his genial temperament and aroused all the dormant barbarism of his nature. Not that in the worst sense Rory became bad; the change in him was more a development of the ancient strain of African character, which had come to him by hereditary descent, but which had needed just this patient drilling by the white man to coax it up to something like ancestral force and quality.

It was a red-letter day for Brimson when at last Rory assumed full equality with him by addressing him as Mr. Brimson. It was done in a manner so superb, too, with a gesture and a bodily pose over-powering to one of Brimson's nervous habit. Rory noted the effect with evident satisfaction, while Brimson felt a fine sense of self-gratulation suffused throughout his diminutive frame. At last he had forced the light of high civilization into the ne-gro's soul, he thought, and henceforth Rory would be a man and a brother, im-bued with all the subtle forces of the most advanced nineteenth-century life.

" No, Mr. Brimson; I cayn't saddle yo' hoss fer yo' any mo', 'ceptin' yo' calls me Mr. Marting," said Rory, with enormous gravity, but with a certain imposing awk-wardness which had its weight.

" Never heerd afore 'at that war yer name," apologized Brimson, as soon as he could find the words.

" Dat's hit; dat's my name. Mr. Marting, sah; Mr. Marting," responded Rory, with great emphasis and pride.

Brimson felt an almost irresistible swell of laughter within him, and, strange to say, along with it an impulse towards lifting his foot and kicking Rory off the veranda. What he did do, however, was to say : —

" Beg parding, Mr. Marting; but ef ye please, sir, fetch out ole Sor'l an' saddle 'im. I hes er notion ter go erp ter the still-house."

Late on the evening following, Brimson returned to his home a pretty badly punished man. He had talked too much to the wrong person on his favorite topic. He was in a desperate mood, which found vent in the most intemperate and sweeping emphasis of his pet opinions.

" 'F I 's er nigger, I 'll be blamed ef I

w'u'd n't rise erp an' jest nat'rally clean erp the whole endoorin' white race!" he raged forth, as he followed Rory down to the little rickety log stable, where old Sorrel was to be housed.

" Dat 's so, Mr. Brimson; dat 's so," said Rory. " Dat 's jest w'at I 's been er mem'-rizin' w'ile yo' be'n gone."

"I 'd rob em; I 'd take the'r lan's, temptations, an' haryditerments; I 'd mek slaves out'n every two-legged one of 'em; I 'd pay 'em back fer the'r meanness an' everlastin' onery cussedness, blame ef I w'u'd n't, Rory," continued the white man.

" Dat 's so, Brimson; dat 's w'at I be'n er-studyin' out w'ile yo' be'n gone ter-day, Brimson," responded Rory.

There was something in his voice which went like a sudden chill through the hot rage of the quondam master.

As when a man has been lost in the woods, and all at once, by a seeming whirl, things right themselves and he knows where he is, Brimson discovered an astonishing but quite natural state of affairs.

Rory unsaddled old Sorrel and put him into the stable; then he came out, shut the door, and said:—

"I's done concluded, Brimson, 'at I's de boss roun' yeah. So yo' mought jes' as well take yo' med'cine right now!"

"W'at—w'at air the matter, Rory?" stammered Brimson.

Rory stretched forth his brawny hand, and, gripping the white man's collar, fairly lifted him from the ground.

"Brimson," he growled, "did n' I tol' yo' ter call me Mr. Marting? Yo''s gwine ter ketch it ef yo' Rory's dis pusson any mo'! Yo' mem'rize dat, will yo'!"

After this Brimson was not seen abroad in the Pine-log region, and for months, perhaps years, little thought was given to him by the people. Often enough Rory was observed going to mill on old Sorrel, or riding to and from the country town;

"CALL ME MR. MARTING"

but no suspicion of the true status over in Sassafras Pocket was aroused until one day Bud Peevy, by merest accident, discovered the whole thing.

He was sitting on a huge fragment of lichen-covered limestone not far from the dim little trail which led into the Pocket. His gun was lying across his knees, and he was fretfully wondering what had become of the brindle cow he had been looking for, when a voice, accompanied by the sound of shuffling feet, came to his ears from some point above him.

" Hit jest do beat de bery debbil how I hab ter w'ar my feets off clean up ter de ankles er-runnin' af'er yo', blame yo' ole hide ! "

The voice was a negro's, strong, soft, vibrant, full of the peculiar African *timbre*. It was resolute, brimming with self-assertion, and yet, in a way, it was suggestive of something like what one might call brutal tenderness. "De bery nex' time 'at yo' runs erway I jes' gwine ter w'ar yo' out!   Ye' see 'f I don', Brimson."

The footfalls came nearer, but the dense foliage shut out from Peevy's view everything more than instantaneous glimpses of the approaching forms of two men.

" Dar 's dat co'n jes' er-gittin' ready ter be hoed, an' dar 's dem dar 'bacco plants jes' ready ter be sot out, an' yar yo' is er-runnin' erway ag'in, dog gone yo' ! "

Peevy craned his long, lean neck to see, if possible, what strange thing was about to appear, but he was not altogether prepared for that which presently emerged from the grove and passed along the little road not a rod from him.

" Git erlong yar, I tol' yo' ! " continued the resonant voice.   " 'Fo' de Lor', I jest erbout cut yo' all ter pieces wid dis yar whorp fust ting yo' knows !   W'a' yo' be'n ter all dis time, anyhow?   Yo' look poorty now, don' yo' ?   S'pose I 's gwine let yo' go er-feeshin' eber' day, does yo' ? "

Peevy noticed that a bluejay in a thorn-bush just beyond the road was preparing to fly away, and by this sign he knew that the men would soon appear.

" W'at I feed yo' fer, an' w'at I furnish yo' dem dar clo's fer, 'ceptin' yo' gwine ter wo'k fer me? Who yo' b'long ter any-how; tell me dat, won't you? Yo' eats mo're 'n ary two peegs an' fo' mules, an' 'en yo' jes' don' want ter wo'k one libin' lick. Bet I 's gwine ter mek yo' fink yo' hide done made out'n red pepper an' smartin'-weeds 'fo' I 's got done wid yo' ! Walk 'long libely."

Certain sharp sounds, as if from heavy blows laid on with a long limber stick or rod, emphasized these vocal perform-ances. Peevy felt a strange thrill run through his nerves. The bluejay sud-denly left its thorn-bush and flew away like a shimmering blue streak through the light mountain air.

" Lif' dem foots libely ; lif' 'em mo' 'an

libely!   Git erp an' waddle, blame yo' ol'
hide, er I jest p'intedly 'll frail de whole
laigs off'n yo' clean up ter yo' gallusses!
Lif' dem foots, I says, er I gwine raise 'em
fer yo' wid dis yar hick'ry, see 'f I don't!"

The first figure that broke from the
dusky cover of the wood was the form of a
small, lean old man, whose thin, white
locks were laid in sleek strands across a
bald spot on his head, and whose high
forehead was wrinkled into a network of
most appealing worry and fright. He
wore no hat, but in one hand he carried
a dilapidated bell-crowned straw tile, while
in the other, tightly clutched, rested a long
cane fishing-rod, from which dangled a
short, much tangled line, and his countenance, drawn, shrunken, and pathetic, ex-
pressed with more power than any form of
words could the dread he felt of the
storming negro behind him.

"I's gwine ter mek de dus' rise out'n yo'
gyarments tell yo' fink some pusson done

built er fire under 'em an' dey 's smokin'
like er tah kiln!"

Along with this gush of vehement rage
out came Rory in close pursuit of the
panting white man, whom Peevy now recognized as Wiley Brimson.

The negro bore in his hand a long, flexible hickory gad, the end of which was
much frayed from the effect of rapid blows
delivered with it on the ground close to
the heels of his scudding victim. The
pursuer was in a state of such concentrated earnestness of purpose that he
looked neither to the right nor to the left,
but held his massive shoulders very high,
at the same time thrusting his head forward
and downward. The tuft of grizzled woolly
beard on his chin was flecked with the
foam of his strenuous scolding. His strides
were melodramatic in their length and
swing, while the collapsed brim of his old
hat flapped energetically to the motion of
his muscular body.

Something poetically savage, like a suggestion from Homer, or like a thought half-expressed by some ancient, rude inscription, beamed from that corrugated African face. Browning might have set such a sketch in verse; Giotto could have fixed it on a panel. Even Peevy was aware of its significance, as the white man, passing him, flung out towards him a quick, appealing, despairing glance.

"Keep yo' nose straight afore yo', er I 's gwine ter wa'm yo' laigs tell yo' feels lak yo' 's er-wadin' in b'ilin' tah up ter yo' wais', wid er red-hot eel er-floppin' roun' yo' blame spindlin' shanks! Git erlong, I tole yo'!"

An indescribable expression came into Peevy's face as he watched this strange procession go by in the direction of Sassafras Pocket and disappear amid the low-hanging sprays of the wood. The voice came bellowing back from time to time, gradually modified by distance and intervening

HE WATCHED THIS STRANGE PROCESSION

objects, until, at last, mellow and far, it had something of lyric softness in its notes.

"Hate ter be erbleeged ter frail de pelt clean off'n yo', Brimson, an' hab yo' gwine roun' yer like er fresh-skinned possum; but ef yo' *will* run erway, w'y, I s'pose I 's got ter let yo' hab it in yarnest. Hustle erlong yah, I tole yo'! I cayn't stan' no foolin'!"

The strokes of the gad upon the ground, given with rhythmical regularity, made a sort of rude counterpoint which added a singular effect to the now but faintly echoing strains.

Presently silence closed in and was not broken till the bluejay came chattering back to its thorn-bush, where it shone like a gem amid the tender green sprays.

Peevy drew a deep breath and began to chuckle reflectively as he rubbed the long, heavy barrel of his gun with his sleeve.

"Jest 'zac'ly as I 'spected," he said to himself, pausing to puff out his gaunt, thinly bearded cheeks; "thet thar nigger hev finally tuk the hint!" He shook his head and shut one eye. "S'pose hit's edication er workin' out!"

Once more Rory's voice, favored by a gentle current of wind, came distinctly back to him.

"Now yo' jes' grab dat hoe poorty libely, ole feller, an' git inter dat co'n patch mighty sudden, er I's gwine ter 'bout finish yo' erp. Drap dat fish-pole, I tole yo'! Drap it, I says!"

Peevy arose and shouldered his gun preparatory to making further and more diligent search for the brindle cow. As he walked away he continued to chuckle at intervals in that dry manner known to mountaineers.

"Hit don't take quite allus ter edicate er nigger; hit air mos'ly er matter o' stickin' ter it, as Brimson hev— Thar's that thar dern cow, now!"

A DUSKY GENIUS

THE founder of a school of thought, the originator of a new strain in art, or the discoverer in the domain of science — any one of these is a tempting subject for an essay; but I hesitate to begin, although I feel sure of the unusual interest that the story of Rack Dillard's life and labors must command. Were it possible to set the man before the world, to be flesh and blood, not even the most cunning art could add to the effect, for Rack Dillard was a genius of no doubtful quality, as a few of the world's keenest intellects have already found out.

He was a black negro slave, illiterate of course, or nearly so; a lover of tobacco; a Baptist in faith, and yet somewhat given to the use of profane language. Presently you shall see that he was the general type of his race,— a personal forecast of the influence to be exerted by slavery upon the civilization which was to follow in the wake of freedom.   His genius was but a slender strain, it is true, and the results of his labors appear slight; but we must keep our standard just while we measure.   He was a slave throughout the flower of his life, drawing not one breath of absolute liberty before he was seventy years old, unable to read or write until after he was seventy-six, and quite ignorant of the simplest elements of mathematics even when he died in triumph at the ripe old age of eighty-three.   And yet he occupies a high place, despite the extreme restrictions and rigid limitations of his life.   You will note that I say a high place *now*, for his elevation, as has been the case too often with genius, was not reached until after his death, which took place in 1872, at his humble little home in Rabun County, Georgia.   Pilgrim

devotees of the new school in art, enthusiastic followers of the latest form of science,
are beginning to make Rack Dillard's
grave a shrine; and the man who owns
the rude cabin where this remarkable negro lived and worked so long is making a
handsome income by demanding of every
visitor a small fee, for the privilege of en-
tering.

Last spring, returning from a sojourn at
Bay Saint Louis, I bent my course so as
to spend a week in the region made classic
by Lanier,—the high hill country through
whose valleys and gorges flow, with here
a purple pool and there a foaming cata-
ract, the two most beautiful rivers in the
world, the Tallulah and the Ulufta. It
was not to verify Lanier's musical description, however, that I went up through the
valleys of Hall into the heart of the Blue
Ridge. The tender jingle of the poet's
rhymes may have been in my ears,—
doubtless it was,—but my thoughts were

busy with the revolution that Rack Dillard had wrought in a certain domain of
art and with the effect he had upon one of
the greatest forces in our civilization. I
felt the picturesqueness, and, if I may say
it, the fitness of the sketch I might make
out of the materials of the old negro's life.
It seemed to me that the world had not
done its duty by him, and that his influence, while it had been made the most of
by a few enthusiasts, had not been properly
acknowledged in a public way. It is true,
as I have said, that certain zealous and
highly enlightened men and women, mostly
Southerners, to their credit be it said, have
formed a quiet but efficient society devoted
to the study of Dillard's, or, as it is usually
called, Rack's philosophy, and some of the
members make pilgrimages to Rack's grave;
still the world has been kept in ignorance
of him for whom the cult exists and by
whom the school was founded.

The mountains of Rabun County are, I

believe, the cerebral part of the great Blue Ridge, the vertebral column, the culmination, the flower of what is, perhaps, the most interesting chain of upheaval in America. The region is an extremely dry, isolated, and lonely one, with every element in its air, its quietude, and its stability of conditions to make it a congenial habitat for Philosophy. Naturally it would be hard for news to escape from such a place, and, besides, mountain people are uncommunicative to an exasperating degree.

That Rack Dillard, the first man of science (both chronologically and in point of eminence) given by the negro race of America — that this preëminent, though illiterate, savant should have spent his whole length of days in the foothills by the rocky banks of the Ulufta, a slave most of the time, — for more than threescore and ten years as I have said, — is a romance which grips the imagination more

engagingly than can any story of trouba-
dour or any chronicle of the age of heroes
and gods.

Dillard's cabin, kept now by a shrewd
Yankee for gain, is reached by a narrow
clay road, slipping away from the pretty
mountain village of Clayton and winding
its course like a brick-red serpent through
a dry, rugged, often picturesque country.
As one advances, the character of the
landscape assumes that composite quality
so attractive to the artist and the geologist.
The road, slowly shrinks, as a river that
loses itself in sand, and at last becomes a
mere shadowy path, leaf-strewn and bough-
shaded, drawn through the stony, brushy,
silent hills to the foot of the mountain
known locally by the appropriate but not
over-euphonious name of the Hog Back.

For some distance before reaching the
Dillard cabin, or, as it is better known,
Rack's house, one follows the course of the
beautiful Ulufta, with the bubbling water

on one side of him and the tumbling, distorted, and rock-pierced foothills on the
other. If he is a sportsman and has
brought his tackle with him, here are pools
and swirls whereon he shall not cast a fly
in vain, since every stone in the stream
has a shadow in which lurks a bass. The
man of science will find much to study on
every hand, and the artist could not ask
for a more varied and fascinating field for
his sketch-book and pencil. As for myself, somewhat given to the practices of
the sportsman, the artist, and the votary of
science, all in turn, not a step of the way
failed to interest me vividly. Looking
back at it now, the little journey fills me
with a sense of the picturesque and the ro-
mantic, touched with a dry, arid, preserva-
tive quality quite indescribable, yet distinct.
The huge fragmentary rocks with their
sear gray lichens worn, like faded rosettes,
upon their imperishable breasts; the trees,
now stunted, now very tall, as the soil

varied or the species alternated, touched
with green and yellowish mosses near the
ground; the sound of the breeze overhead,
and the murmur of the river here or a
spring-stream there; the fragrance of opening buds and springing spathes; the
voices of birds, many of them migrants,
like myself, dallying for a day or two —
all these, with glimpses of high precipices
and far blue peaks, the whole overarched
with a tender, almost violet sky, linger
with me, as vague as a dream, as real as
the furniture in my study, making up one
of the most striking and perpetually differentiated impressions set in my memory.

When at last one turns aside from what
by courtesy is the main road, he approaches
Dillard's cabin from the west, the gravelly
bed of a bright brooklet serving as guide.
The structure appears to lean for support
against the face of a perpendicular cliff
whose fringe of cedars, stunted and gnarled,
overtops the decaying and mossy roof that

slants forward so as to cover a rude porch
or veranda in front, near which stands the
stump of an old mulberry-tree. Thanks
to the keen business sense of the Yankee,
the place has been kept just as Rack left
it, with all its furniture and belongings
intact.

From the cabin door a well-worn path
curves round the corner of the escarpment
and turns over the hill-spur to the much
more pretentious dwelling formerly owned
and occupied by Rack's master, Judge
Spivey Dillard, a somewhat eccentric man,
who during the latter part of his life devoted all his time in a way to biological
investigations and to reading the works of
Darwin, Owen, Macgillivray, and Alfred
Wallace. He was a bachelor, living alone,
surrounded with such luxury as he cared
for, leaving to his slaves the management
of a valuable plantation in bottom lands of
the Ulufta River.

Rack was about sixty years old when

his master retired him from active field work and permitted him to assume the lighter duties of a house servant — a man of chores, to come from his cabin at any moment, day or night, rain or shine, whenever the judge blew a blast upon a small tin horn kept for the purpose.

Doubtless it was from his master, who as his years increased became more and more inclined to scientific garrulousness, that Rack caught the first suggestion which led to his singular, and under the circumstances successful, career in a slender but interesting course of science and art.

The earliest intimation of the negro's work in his chosen line came to the judge one day when he blew his horn and for the first time Rack failed to answer the summons. A second blast had no better effect, and a third echoed away through the woods without response. Judge Dillard felt sure that his faithful servant had

JUDGE DILLARD

met with some ill, and acting upon the moment's impulse, hastened over to Rack's cabin, where he found the old fellow in a rapt state, seated on his sheepskin stool under the then flourishing mulberry-tree. The judge thought that Rack was asleep; the suggestion engendered rage.

"Rack, what do you mean here, you lazy old lubber you? I'll wear you as thin as a hand-saw in half a minute!" he exclaimed, rushing upon the negro and shaking him till he fairly rattled.

Rack bounced up and drew in a deep, gasping breath.

"Why didn't you answer that horn, you old vagabond?" continued the judge, giving Rack two or three resounding cuffs. "Tell me, or I'll mash every ultimate molecule in the tissues of your body!"

Rack dodged, grunted, and gasped again, getting his breath as a man who comes out of a plunge in cold water.

"Lost your tongue, have you?" the judge

went on, still cuffing vigorously. "I 'll
stir up your nerve-cells and jar your gan-
glions into activity; I 'll knock all your
foramens into one; I 'll make magma of
you; I 'll reduce you to protoplasmic
pulp!"

The negro soon got himself together,
and tore away from his master's grasp.
His voice came to him at the same time,
and it was no child's voice.

"Stop dat! stop dat!" he exclaimed,
dodging meantime sundry blows and kicks.
" Yo' don' know w'at yo' doin', Mars' Spivey; 'fo' de Lor', yo' don'!"

But the judge did not stop until quite
out of breath and otherwise exhausted.
He had managed to hurt himself much
more than he had punished the negro, and
now, panting and glaring, he sank upon
the stool, his grizzled beard quivering and
his hat awry.

" I 's pow'ful s'prise at yo', Mars' Spivey;
'fo' Gor, I is," Rack remarked, wiping the

perspiration from his face with his sleeve, while, with his feet apart, he squared himself in front of the judge. " W'en yo' bu's' in on dat ca'c'lation o' mine, yo' jes' eberlastin' did play de bery debil wid er 'vestigation ob science, I tell yo'."

Judge Dillard's fiery eyes, still bent upon his servant's face, shot forth a queer gleam as Rack uttered the word " science." Probably if he had not been so very blown and tired he would have renewed his assault and battery, but the sheepskin stool, with its deep, soft fleece, was a restful seat.

" W'en yo' begin yo' wo'k onto me jes' now," Rack went on, " er-thumpin' me ober de head, an' er-whangin' me in de face an' eyes, an' er-jerkin' de bery liver and lights out'n me, I 's jes' at dat time ready ter re'ch fo' a 'clusion in biorology, an' yo' knock it plumb frough me an' stomp it inter de ye'th."

By this time the judge had recollected what it was that he wanted of Rack.

"You just biology off to the stable, and take Bald Eagle" — that was his saddle-horse — "over to the blacksmith's shop and have his shoes reset, and, Rack, the very next time that you go to sleep and don't hear my horn I'll take you down country and sell you, see if I don't!" He delivered this order, set with the sting of the most terrible threat known to an up-country slave, in a tone which made Rack's soul shiver. The negro stood not on the manner of his going, but went forthwith to do the task assigned him.

Judge Dillard remained on the soft stool, and, leaning his head against the cool bark of the mulberry-tree, gazed idly up into the thick, dark foliage, now splashed with the soft purple of ripening berries. His recent exertion and excitement had left him quite averse to further physical or mental effort; indeed, the reaction gradually engendered in him that dreamy, misty mood which in its soothing restfulness is next to sleep.

A woodpecker, with a black jacket and a scarlet head, came and alighted on a corner of the cabin roof where a course projected. It eyed the judge a moment, then beat a fine rolling tattoo on the resonant end of a warped board. The sound was a peculiar one, double in its nature, the second or undertone being a strange, vibrant strain, sweet as the softest note of flute or violin. The judge's ears were in just the most receptive condition; the vague, sweet ringing chord flowed in and spread throughout his senses. A mocking-bird had been flitting about in the mulberry-tree overhead, and the judge noticed that it had the peculiar habit of fetching mulberries to a certain point on a stout bough, where it thrust them into a small pit or knot-hole, and, after churning them for a little while with its beak, drank their rich subacid juice.

To the half-dreaming man of science observations of this nature were distantly suggestive. His lips moved, and he murmured, "Strange that while the harsh-voiced *melanerpes erythrocephalus* is drawing aboriginal music from a fragment of *pinus mitis*, the silver-tongued *mimus polyglottus* is content to make cider from the insipid fruit of *morus rubra*." At the sound of his words both birds flew away as if terribly frightened.

The judge was a good-hearted man, though rather hasty-tempered, and when his calmer mind began to contemplate the treatment given Rack a while ago, a twinge of remorse shot through it. He recalled, with a vague sense of its extreme novelty, the fact that Rack had claimed, and with intense seriousness, that his lapse from duty had been owing to complete absorption in a scientific investigation. The judge chuckled heartily, then became grave, as the phases of the situation passed from ludicrous to pathetic. What if, after all, a negro could comprehend and follow the golden threads of biological study?

What if he, Judge Spivey Dillard, jurist
and scientist, had thumped and cuffed and
pounded a man, black though he was and
born slave, just at the moment when a
mystery of life was beginning to make itself comprehensible to his understanding?
The thought was heavy with suggestions
over which the judge pondered deep and
long; then he slept, leaning heavily against
the tree, while the dry mountain air fanned
his furrowed face and shook the grizzled
beard that fringed his lank jaws and protruding chin. Through his slumber fell
the sweet bouquet of the luscious berries
and the tender rustle of the broad leaves.
The woodpecker returned again and again
to sound a bar or two of his queer music
on the old warped board, and the mocking-bird ventured back to the little pit
wherein he churned his mulberries and
made his fragrant wine.

Judge Dillard awoke just as Rack came
shuffling down the path, returning from

doing his errand.   The old gentleman heard the familiar footfalls, rubbed his eyes, yawned, and stretched himself.   Rack, lifting both hands and expanding his eyes dramatically, exclaimed : —

" Well, 'fo' de Lor', Mars' Spivey! yo' loungin' roun' yer yit?   Wha' gwine happen nex', I wonder?   Been 'sleep all dis time?"

The judge yawned again, but he was eyeing Rack keenly, as if to look through and through him.   The old slave noted this with misgiving, secretly fearing, indeed, that something was going to be said on the subject of a hand of fine leaf tobacco that he had surreptitiously abstracted from his master's store not long since; but the judge merely remarked that he had been feeling a trifle drowsy, and then added : —

" Sit down there, Rack," indicating a corner of the porch-floor.   " I want to interrogate you touching biology."

It would be tedious and quite uninstructive to insert here the long dialogue that ensued between the judge and his slave. The almost unpronounceable words, the Greek and Latin phrases, and the Darwinian quotations indulged in by the white man, were thoroughly equilibrated by the savage interpretation of them rendered by the negro. To say that Rack reveled in the conversation would be but a shadowy expression of the truth. Indeed, his enjoyment was ecstatic, even excruciating, as was proved by his bodily writhing and his facial contortions. For how many long years had he been furtively catching detached bits of his master's learning, growing hungrier and thirstier day by day for the full draught he was now taking in! Every precious word of the jargon of science caught by his ears had been held in the tenacious grip of memory. He had crooned over them in the depth of the night; he had sung them in the field; he had conned them while hunting the famous 'possum of the Ulufta valley, until they had entered into the innermost fibres of his life, so to speak, and been assimilated perfectly without being in the least digested.

Nor was Judge Spivey Dillard less charmed than his slave with the occasion current. He came near forgetting to ask Rack for further explanation of the alleged investigation which had led to the recent encounter; but he caught himself just in time. Rack was ready, nay eager to enlighten his master.

"Well, sah, Mars' Spivey," he began, crossing his index fingers in front of him, "dat wa' er ques'ion ob de general aberage ob ci'cumstances; or, speakin' mo' plainer, it wa' jes' dis: what air de biorology ob de singin'-boa'd, an' er mockin'-bird 'at feeds er mu'berry limb, an' er' possum w'at go out, jes' like er can'le w'en yo' blow it?"

The judge, more from long habit than

from any desire to have this apparently absurd proposition simplified, straightened himself up a little, and said : —

"Repeat that statement, Rack."

" Ce'tainly, sah, ce'tainly ; I gwine mek it reas'n'ble ter yo' gum'tion, 'mejetly, sah," responded the negro, lifting one forefinger and tapping the other with it.

"It 's dis here way : dey 's er dry old boa'd 'at kin sing er chune ; dey 's er mockin'-bird w'at feeds er mu'berry limb ; an' dey 's er wollopin' great big old 'possum 'at kin jes fade right out an' tu'n hese'f inter nothin' w'ile yo' 's er-lookin' at 'im. Dat 's w'at I done been er-'vestigatin' w'en yo' try ter tah me all ter pieces dis mo'nin' ; an' jes as yo' light onter me I was er-j'in-in' dem fac's tergedder an' jes' er-re'chin' out fo' de aberage ob 'im. Mighty sorry yo' do dat, Mars' Spivey ; it gwine ter be er great loss ter biorology, sah, sho 's yo' bo'n, sah."

The judge was disgusted in one sense,

and in another he was, strange to say,
deeply interested. He was curious to
know just what Rack meant by a singing-
board, a mocking-bird that fed a mulberry limb, and a 'possum that could ren-
der itself invisible at will. Pursuing this
curiosity, he catechized the negro after
the artful manner of a lawyer to the business born. Rack was slow to give up his
secret, but, bit by bit, the judge drew out
the whole of it. The singing-board was
the one in the cabin's roof upon which
the woodpecker beat its long roll in the
morning. The under-hum of that sonorous piece of wood was still softly rever-
berating in the judge's ears. The mocking-bird that fed the limb was the one that
the judge himself had seen churning mulberries to pulp in the opening on the
bough overhead; but the 'possum that
could fade out and disappear had been met
by no man save Rack. And what a 'possum it was! — as large as a six-months-

old pig, with a tail quite a yard long, and
a nose that turned up almost at right angles. Time and again Rack had come
upon this magnificent animal down in the
Ulufta bottoms, where the timber was
thick and heavy; but he could by no art
known to the 'possum-hunter capture it,
for the reason that it invariably faded away
to nothing, as ghosts are said to do, leaving only a faint, wan light flickering for a
moment where it had been.

Somehow when Rack, in his simple
dialect, related how for more than twenty
years he had lain in his lowly bed of morn-
ings listening to the strange, sweet vibra-
tions of that singing-board; and how for
the same period, during every year's mulberry season, he had watched the mocking-
bird stuff the fruit into the hole in that
limb; and, more than all, how for a score
of autumns and winters he had used every
means at command to capture that wonderful 'possum, it got the judge's imagina-

tion aroused and set his memory to work.
His long-lost youth brought up a host of
experiences left fifty years behind, and
among them hunting the 'possum was perhaps the raciest and most barbaric. Those
were the days when a persimmon had exquisite flavor, and when muscadines were
better than any garden· grape. For a
while he tasted over again the far-away
sweets of boyhood; smelt the keen fragrance; saw the gay colors; heard the
ravishing sounds; felt the thrill of vigorous, buoyant, untainted life. Elusive, pun-
gent reminiscences came in and wandered
through his mind like bees through an old
weed-grown flower-bed.

"Yes, sah, yo' busted up er powerfu'
close ca'c'lation by yo' onreson'ble savage-
rousness dis mo'nin', Mars' Spivey," insisted Rack, shaking his head dolefully,
and ending with a long, deep sigh of re-
gret. "Yo' onj'inted my 'magination."

This touched the judge, for at the moment he was fixing one of those shadowy half-remembrances. Surely it was so — yes, it was so — he vaguely recollected — yes, once, long years ago, an opossum had disappeared mysteriously right before his eyes. The animal was at the time hanging by its tail to the low, full-fruited bough of a persimmon-tree; he approached it with a club, when, lo! it faded away and was gone. Now he described the incident to Rack, who received it with delight, and from that day forward the two men discussed at intervals the possibility of a marsupial's having the power of self-elimination under great stress of danger. For some time the negro was chiefly a listener, while his master, seated in a deep chair on the stoop of the mansion, dilated with much show of learning upon the isolated position of the opossum family in the animal kingdom. The judge had a theory of his own, to the effect that a 'possum represented humor of a more or less comic sort, and he explained to Rack that it was the 'possum-eating habit among the negroes of the South which had given them their sense of barbaric comedy and their love of humorous music.

"It is nothing in the world but 'possum-fat," said he, "that has made such idiots of you niggers. It makes your heads wag, and your hands pat, and your feet dance; it makes you laugh at everything, and act the fool generally. In short, Rack, 'possum-fat is the essential oil of tomfoolery and buffoonery and absurd comicality."

But Rack was longing for a scientific explanation of the singing-board and the limb-feeding mocking-bird.

"But there is no correlation between these simple things and the opossum question,— no correlation whatever, Rack," the judge explained.

"But I say dey is," asserted Rack, with a vehemence that fairly startled his master. "Dey is er corroliation, so dey is, an'

dat jes' w'a' I gwine show yo' w'en yo' try
ter tah me up."

" Rack, I say that there is no correlation
whatever," replied the judge.

" Dey is — dey is, I tell yo'," retorted
Rack.

The judge reached for his cane, and the
negro bolted away, as if shot from a war-
wolf, his big flat feet pounding the path
with rapid and resounding strokes until
the cabin was reached.

Rack's memory was remarkable. He
kept in mind the 'possum theory advanced
by his master, and it grew upon him day
by day, apropos of which he went about
singing the old quatrain : —

> " W'en de ole 'possum gwine ter run,
> His hide jes' nat'ly bu'st wid fun ;
> Ef nigger knock 'im on de head,
> He still keep grinnin' w'en he dead ! "

Many times the same question arose as
to the possibility of a correlation between
the singing-board, the mocking-bird that

fed the mulberry limb, and the opossum that could disappear at will; but the disagreement of master and slave was, it appeared, unsurmountable. The judge finally formulated his proposition thus: "There cannot possibly exist any correlation whatever between a self-eliminating *didelphys virginiana*, a berry-eating *mimus polyglottus*, and a dry fragment of *pinus mitis* struck by the mandibles of *melanerpes erythrocephalus*."

Rack was staggered, but he shook his head doggedly, and responded with exasperating brevity, "I say dey is."

From the very nature of things it came to pass that this problem in science occupied every moment of Rack's gradually increasing leisure. To solve it, and so triumph over his master, would be a crowning glory. The nebulous beginning of a solution was, in fact, forming itself like a milky way across his mind. The judge himself was so keenly pleased with his old slave's

mysterious ambition that he almost wished
him to succeed, even if it should appear
thereby that color had won precisely at the
point where color always had been supposed to be weakest. Rack's enthusiasm
and zeal were tempered all the time with
such grotesque and comical humor, and
accompanied with facial contortions so expressive of savage wisdom, that a kind of
infection exhaled therefrom and insinuated
itself into the judge's imagination.

As time flew on — and how it does fly
as the evening of life draws toward night!
— Rack, while growing more and more
confident of success, became very reticent
as to the progress of his investigations.
Finally the judge discovered that something of a secret nature was in progress
down at the cabin. He questioned Rack
on the subject, but received no satisfaction,
and when he threatened and menaced the
old fellow he was reminded that a most in-
opportune assault once before had delayed
the great investigation.

"Cou'se you kin jump on ter me an' w'ar me out, Mars' Spivey," said he dolefully and with a lugubrious twist of his strong African face, "but ef yo' does it's gwine set biorology back jes' fifteen yeahs an' fo' days mo', sho 's you 's borned, Mars' Spivey, dat's w'at it's er-gwine ter do. Jes' fifteen yeahs an' fo' days mo'."

"But, Rack, what upon earth is your objection to telling me?" demanded the judge, with querulous and helpless insistence.

Rack looked sidewise at his master, with a suspicious and over-cunning leer in his milky old eyes.

"Da' now, Mars' Spivey," he said, chuckling in a low falsetto, — "da' now, yo' know jes' es well es I does dat it not gwine ter do fo' one scientist ter tell 'nodder scientist any ob his disciberies afo' he git 'em fastened solid in he mind, er he steal 'em, sho 's yo' borned. Don't yo' ricomember w'en yo' read ter me in de book 'bout

seberal 'markable ins'ances ob dat sort er
misplaced co'fidence? Ya', sah, yo' did,
Mars' Spivey. Now den, yo' 's er scientist, ain't yo'? Well, I is too, an' I jes'
know mighty well what yo' 'd do. Yo' 'd
steal my discibery, an' jes' tu'n roun' an'
sw'ar 'at it 's yo'n! No, sah, Mars' Spivey,
yo' don' come dat game. I 's not quite er
eejit yit!"

Rack had his way, and the judge was
both tantalized and delighted, while the
days flew by like birds before a storm.

Year followed year, bringing no notable
change in the dry, stony mountain landscape. The dessicative influence of the
climate preserved things *in statu quo*. At
length the great war came on; it rolled its
heavy echoes over the blue peaks to the
north and west of them, but neither master
nor slave heeded them much; for the tie
that bound these two old men together
was stronger than the proclamation of a
President or any amendment to the Amer-

ican Constitution. They became more
and more attached to each other, the negro in the latter years gradually assuming
the stronger part, while the judge, whose
mind and body, weakening together, appeared to be slowly drying up, gave most
of his time to watching the tedious progress of Rack's investigation.

It was one fine morning in December,
1865. The previous night had been a
clear, sharp, frosty one, crisping the late
greenery of the sturdy mountain oaks and
making mellow and luscious the persim-
mons of the Ulufta valley. The judge
was on his veranda, smoking his pipe in
the sunshine, and enjoying the soft color
show set against the steep slope of the
Hog Back, when Rack shambled up the
steps and began dancing on the floor, his
heavy shoes making a mighty racket.

"I 's got ter de eend! I 's got to de
eend!" he sang out. "I done 'sciber de
corroliation ob de boa'd an' de mocking-

bird an' de 'possum, an' I done settle de
'vestigation, Mars' Spivey; ef I hain't den
de debil 's er co'n dodger! "

Before the judge could recover from the
surprise of the occasion, Rack changed
the step of his dance to a fluttering and
rattling double-shuffle as an accompaniment in counterpoint to the following
snatch of song: —

> " De mockin'-bird fink it smart o' him
>   W'en he hide he music in de limb!
>   Oh, ya, ya, ya!
>   An' er wha, wha, wha!
>   W'en he stuff he chunes all in de limb !

> " Dat pine boa'd sing till it wa'p right roun',
>   An' ebery day it ketch mo' soun'.
>   Oh, ya, ya, ya!
>   An' er wha, wha, wha!
>   Fo' ebery day it ketch mo' soun'!

> " De 'possum gwine ter shed he skin,
>   An' den de music will begin.
>   Oh, ya, ya, ya!
>   An' er wha, wha, wha!
>   W'en dat ole 'possum shed he skin ! "

He ended with a high fling and a tremendous foot-stroke on the resounding floor. The judge remonstrated and even tried the old worn threats, but Rack would not be controlled.

"I done cotch onter de corroliation ob de biorology!" he cried exultingly, still skipping about. "Dat man Dahwin, he plumb dead-right ebery time on de biorology an' devolution. It gwine ter be er cla'r case ob nat'ral dejection an' de 'vival ob de fitified! It gwine ter be er cla'r case ob devolution f'om de gin'ral ter de spec'fication, f'om de simple ter de confound! Free ob de simplest an' no'-countest gineralist fings in de worl' gwine ter be devoluted inter de one confoundest specialest best t'ing 'at eber yo' see in all yo' bo'n days!"

Here he caught the double-shuffle again, and added to it what was known as the chicken-peck back-step.

"I kill dat ole 'possum las' night," he

added in a calmer way, though he was panting heavily. "Hi! 'fo' Gor, I jes' knock 'im lim'er wid er light-'ood knot, an' skin 'im afore he done kickin'. Bless yo' life, Mars' Spivey, but dat's de bigges' 'possum-skin dis yer chile eber see in he whole bo'n days. Look mos' like er calf-hide er-hangin' down dah on my doo'."

A few days after this the judge was surprised to discover that Rack had climbed up in the mulberry-tree and cut off the famous limb which had been fed for so many fruitful summers by the mocking-bird. The resonant board, too, had been removed from the cabin's roof.

Now came the six long years of patient labor by which Rack Dillard reached the goal of his soul's ambition. First he hung a section of the mulberry limb, about three feet long, close to the jamb of his fireplace to season, and then he began with a piece of glass scraping thinner the old warped board. Meantime the opossum's skin was lying under a bed of hickory ashes, which sooner or later would deprive it of its hair.

Day after day, through the seasons and the years, the old judge found his chief pleasure in sitting with his pipe in his mouth, watching Rack scrape and file and cut and carve the singing-board and the full-fed mulberry billet, or manipulate the pale, translucent hide of the opossum.

" I 'll jes' show yo' 'bout de corroliation ob dem fings, Mars' Spivey," the negro would mutter, without lifting his bleared and sunken eyes. " Yo' said dey was n't no corroliation 'tween 'em, an' I said dey was. Pooty soon we see who gwine be right 'bout dis yer biorology question, so we will."

The singing-board proved to be a singularly even-fibred piece of pine three feet long and four inches wide by a half-inch thick. For about fifty years it had lain in the cabin roof absorbing the warmth of the sun and the drying sweetness of the mountain wind. Slowly its tissue had been granulated and rearranged under the daily jarring of the woodpecker's bill, until now, after the scraping and polishing Rack had given it, the wood had an amber, waxen appearance, and was flexible and sonorous as the finest tempered steel. But the mulberry billet! Never was there another such a bit of color, fragrance, and fineness. From the gnarled little pit, in which for fifty years the mocking-bird had brewed his purple wine, the rich stain of the berries had spread through the wood in a waving, rippling flood, giving it a royal dye and a fruity, musty odor like the bouquet of old wine.

Near the close of the six-years' period mentioned awhile ago, Rack, on the lookout for his master's daily visit, met the judge at the cabin door, and remarked: —

" 'Bleeged ter say ter yo', Mars' Spivey, 'at yo' 's not welcome ter-day. Yo' got no business down yer nohow."

The judge was taken by surprise. He leaned on his staff and looked quizzically into the old negro's face. Rack did not relent.

"Yo''s not gwine inside er dat cabin dis day," he persisted, "'ca'se I's got ter hab de room all ter myse'f. I's er-gittin' ter de corroliation w'at we been er'sputin' er-bout, an' I's jes eberlastin'ly er-knockin' de holy stuffin' out'n all yo' ram'fications on de biorology. So yo' kin jes' go back, honey, an' wait tell I come fo' yo'. No, I's not gwine come fo' yo' nudder; yo' jes' come yo' own se'f nex' Sat'd'y night. Yo' heah, now? Nex' Sat'd'y night I's gwineter be ready fo' yo'."

The judge turned about slowly and reluctantly; leaned a moment on his cane; faltered when he tried to say something; then trudged back to his favorite seat on the mansion's stoop, where he smoked and dozed. Recently his age had been softening his feelings. An hysterical sentimen-

tality had gained upon him. Rack's re-
fusal to confide in him had worn upon
him day by day for years, and now he felt,
however indefinitely, that the last straw of
ingratitude had been heaped upon him.
Nevertheless he waited patiently for Saturday evening to come, with but the
slightest and vaguest sense of the olden-
time arrogance which would have resented
the merest suggestion of being dictated to
by a negro. This supremacy gained over
his lifelong master was, it seems to me,
the highest evidence of Rack Dillard's
genius.

When Saturday afternoon faded at last
into twilight, which in turn slowly softened into a moonlight night, the judge
began to make some preliminary movements with a view to visiting the cabin;
but he lingered, cane in hand and pipe in
mouth, at the little gate before his house,
hesitating for no particular reason. It
was midsummer, and the dry softness of

the mountain air touched tenderly the dreaming, dusky leaf-masses of the woods, and hung misty veils on the horizon. He presently crept through the gate, hesitating just outside for a while, and gazing up at the stars and the moon. It was his way of restraining his impatience, and besides he had not been quite able to forgive Rack. He toddled along the path, fitfully pausing here and there, until at last he turned the corner of the rock. At the cabin porch he stopped short and stood in a listening attitude, amazed at first and then entranced. The little house was full of music that rippled out through every opening, and tinkled away in thin rills along the dim paths of the woods. The judge remembered that in his young days Rack had been a musician of no mean ability; but for years he had had no instrument to play upon. Evidently he was now making up for lost time; and what music! Was ever anything else so bur-

dened with pathos ? So barbaric, still so
refined ? So brimming with virile force,
so tender, so touching, so hilarious, so
comic, so sweet, so true ? The old judge
felt the hot tears gush up into his eyes,
he knew not why. It was as if the old
times of his boyhood had blown their
sweets back upon him, with the laughter
of childhood, the patter and shuffle of
dancing feet, the songs of myriad mock-
ing-birds, the rustle of satin leaves and
silken wings, the bubble and bouquet of
purple wine, the fragrance and resonance
of all the sweet, dry, sun-seasoned wood
that ever was wrought into violin or harp.
He stood there crying and laughing, keep-
ing time with his staff and wagging his
head, now slowly, now briskly, as the
strains varied from grave to gay.

> "Oh, de peckerwood he head er red,
>   Lolly, lally, ho!"

came forth Rack's voice, rich and strong
despite old age, singing to a well-timed

accompaniment and the pat, pat, pat of his
shoe.

> " Oh, de peckerwood he head er red.
>   Lolly, lally, ho !
>   An' de mockin'-bird he been stall-fed,
>   Lolly, lally, ho !

> " Oh, de 'possum am er funny t'ing,
>   Lolly, lally, ho !
>   W'en he lif' 'is foot fo' de pigeon-wing,
>   Lolly, lally, ho !

> " De pine boa'd set my notion gwine,
>   Lolly, lally, ho !
>   An' de mulberry limb it mighty fine,
>   Lolly, lally, ho ! "

The judge could bear it no longer.   He
pushed open the door and went in.   Rack
looked up and nodded, but kept on singing and playing, emphasizing his notes
more than ever, if that were possible.
Judge Dillard began to dance, and even to
sing, as Rack changed the tune : —

> " Oh, lo'dy massy, how d' yo' feel,
>   Wid de' 'possum grease down in yo' heel,
>   An' yo' head all full o' turnip-pie,
>   An' er big sweet 'tater in yo' eye ? "

The negro's voice ceased when the judge's began, but the banjo, quickening the new air, rang on in jolly unison. Who would have thought that an octogenarian could ever have danced like that!

> " Wash yo' teef wid de blackin'-brush,
>   Grease yo' ha'r in er pot er mush,
>   Go to de dance er Sat'd'y night,
>   Patrol whop yo' 'fo' daylight ! "

The black had conquered the white. When the judge sank at last into a chair he was exhausted, panting, sweating, his heart beating violently. Rack keyed one string up a trifle, leaned a little farther over, and began to sing plaintively: —

> " Marster, now we 's growin' ole,
>   De heads am white, de feet am cole,
>   But de ole, ole age cayn't do no harm
>   W'en de heart, de heart am true an' warm.

> " Marster, w'en we drop ter sleep,
>   In de grabe so cool an' deep,
>   Den we nebber feel de storm,
>   Ef our po' ole hearts is warm."

They sat up all night long, now singing, now dancing, anon talking over old times on the Ulufta. Something in the music of that banjo had an intoxicating effect. Judge Dillard felt fifty years younger, and Rack found it not in the least difficult or tiresome to play for an hour at a time without a moment's rest. The exquisite odor of the pine wood touched the air in the room, and there was a distinct flavor of ripe mulberries straying elusively about.

When I visited Rack's cabin I examined with care and interest the incomparable banjo which the negro's patient genius had built out of the "singing-board, the over-fed mulberry limb, and the skin of the famous Ulufta 'possum," as the thrifty Yankee proprietor describes it. No one can doubt that science and art were happily married in the making of that superb instrument. A glance shows that the carving, the proportions of the parts, and the fine details of the finishing — from the silvery, translucent skin that covers the head, to the rich purple of the mulberry neck, and the gold-colored hoop fashioned out of the old warped board that had sung so long in the cabin roof — are exquisite beyond description. On the under part of the neck is the only authentic autograph left by Rack Dillard. It is a legible carved inscription of four words : " Dis is de corroliation."

Rack's grave is on the top of the high cliff above his cabin. It overlooks the lovely valley of the Ulufta, and commands a fine view of the Hog Back. To this high tomb of the great negro originator of true dialect, romance, and minstrelsy, have come, as pilgrims to a shrine, many faithful and devoted students to pay their respects to the founder of their school. Wreaths of flowers are laid tenderly on the mound, and in the bold escarpment of the rocks are cut ineffaceably some names beloved of all men. Among these, and high in the list, I noticed with peculiar pleasure Joel Chandler Harris, H. S. Edwards, Thomas Nelson Page, and Irwin Russell, — the names of men whose stories and songs and sketches have made known to the world the tender faithful heart, the rich, sunny humor, and the deeper soul qualities of the Southern negro. I hesitated awhile ; then, where no one would be apt to see it, I scrawled my own signature to testify that I too had been there.

Rack must have been a genius, a high type of his race. As in the case of every other genius, he foresaid or forecast the life that was to come after him, while at the same time he was the exponent of the past. His songs and his banjo strains left in the brisk, sweet air of the New South a lasting reminder of the old plantation days. The years he spent so patiently in establishing a close relationship among his materials, and which drew together the three elements of his art, fun, pathos, and music, have served well the civilization of our time, and have added a distinct tint and a new flavor to life. We owe a great deal to Rack Dillard. Peace to his ashes!

THE BALANCE OF POWER

" I DON'T hesitate to say to you that I regard him as but a small remove in nature from absolute trash, Phyllis, — absolute trash. His character may be good — doubtless it is; but he is not of good family, and he shows it. What is he but a mountain cracker? There is no middle ground; trash is trash!"

Colonel Mobley Sommerton spoke in a rich bass voice, slowly rolling his words. The bagging of his trousers at the knees made his straight legs appear bent, as if for a jump at something, while his daughter Phyllis looked at him searchingly, but not in the least impatiently, her fine gray eyes wide open, and her face, with its delicately blooming cheeks, its peach-petal lips, and its saucy little nose, all attention and half-indignant surprise.

"Of course," the colonel went on, with a conciliatory touch in his words, when he had waited some time for his daughter to speak and she spoke not, — "of course you do not care a straw for him, Phyllis; I know that the daughter of a Sommerton could n't care for such a " —

"I don't mind saying to you that I do care for him, and that I love him, and want to marry him," broke in Phyllis, with tremulous vehemence, tears gushing from her eyes at the same time; and a depth of touching pathos seemed to open behind her words, albeit they rang like so many notes of rank boldness in the old man's ears.

"Phyllis!" he exclaimed. Then he stooped a little, his trousers bagging still more, and he stood in an attitude almost stagy, a flare of choleric surprise leaping into his face. "Phyllis Sommerton, what *do* you mean? Are you crazy? You say that to me?"

The girl — she was just eighteen — faced her father with a look at once tearfully saucy and lovingly firm. The sauciness, however, was superficial and physical, not in any degree a part of her mental mood. She could not, had she tried, have been the least bit willful or impertinent with her father, who had always been a model of tenderness. Besides, a girl never lived who loved a parent more unreservedly than Phyllis loved Colonel Sommerton.

"Go to your room, miss! go to your room! Step lively at that, and let me have no more of this nonsense. Go! I command you!"

The stamp with which the colonel's rather substantial boot just then shook the floor seemed to generate some current of force sufficient to whirl Phyllis about and send her upstairs in an old-fashioned fit of hysteria. She was crying and talking and running all at the same time, her voice made liquid like a bird's, and yet jangling with mixed emotions. Down fell her wavy long brown hair almost to her feet, one rich strand trailing over the rail, as she mounted the steps, while the rustling of her muslin dress told off the springy motion of her limbs till she disappeared in the gilt-papered gloom aloft, where the windowless hall turned at right angles with the stairway.

Colonel Sommerton was smiling grimly by this time, and his iron-gray moustache quivered humorously.

" She 's a little brick," he muttered; " a chip off the old log — by zounds, she is! She means business. Got the bit in her teeth, and fairly splitting the air!" He chuckled raucously. " Let her go: she 'll soon tire out."

Sommerton Place, a picturesque old mansion, as mansions have always gone in north Georgia, stood in a grove of oaks on a hilltop overlooking a little mountain town, beyond which uprose a crescent of blue peaks against a dreamy summer sky. Behind the house a broad plantation rolled its billow-like ridges of corn and cotton.

The colonel went out on the veranda and lit a cigar, after breaking two or three matches that he nervously scratched on a column.

This was the first quarrel that he had ever had with Phyllis.

Mrs. Sommerton had died when Phyllis was twelve years old, leaving the little girl to be brought up in a boarding-school in Atlanta. The widowed man did not marry again, and when his daughter came home six months before the opening of our story, it was natural that he should see nothing but loveliness in the fair, bright, only child of his happy wedded life, now ended forever.

The reader must have taken for granted

that the person under discussion in the conversation touched upon at the outset of this writing was a young man; but Tom Banister stood for more than the sum of the average young man's values. He was what in our republic is recognized as a promising fellow, bright, magnetic, shifty, well forward in the neologies of society, business, and politics, a born leader in a small way, and as ambitious as poverty and a brimming self-esteem could make him. From his humble law-office window he had seen Phyllis pass along the street in the old Sommerton carriage, and had fallen in love as promptly as possible with her plump, lissome form and pretty face.

He sought her acquaintance, avoided with cleverness a number of annoying barriers, assaulted her heart, and won it, all of which stood as mere play when compared with climbing over the pride and prejudice of Colonel Sommerton.   For

Banister was nobody in a social way, as viewed from the lofty top of the hill at Sommerton Place ; indeed, all of his kins-people were mountaineers, honest, it is true, but decidedly woodsy, who tilled stony acres in a pocket beyond the first blue ridge yonder. His education seemed good, but it had been snatched from the books by force, with the savage certainty of grip which belongs to genius.

Colonel Sommerton, having unbounded confidence in Phyllis's aristocratic breed-ing, would not open his eyes to the atti-tude of the young people, until suddenly it came into his head that possibly the al-most briefless plebeian lawyer had ulterior designs while climbing the hill, as he was doing noticeably often, from town to Som-merton Place. But when this thought arrived the colonel was prompt to act. He called up the subject at once, and we have seen the close of his interview with Phyllis.

Now he stood on the veranda and puffed his cigar with quick short draughts, as a man does who falters between two horns of a dilemma. He turned his head to one side, as if listening to his own thoughts, his tall pointed collar meantime fitting snugly in a crease of his furrowed jaw.

At this moment the shambling, yet in a way facile footsteps of Barnaby, the sporadic freedman of the household, were soothing. Colonel Sommerton turned his eyes on the comer inquiringly, almost eagerly.

"Well, Barn, you're back," he said.

"Yah, sah; I's had er confab wid 'em," remarked the negro, seating himself on the top step of the veranda, and mopping his coal-black face with a red cotton handkerchief; "an' hit do beat all. Niggahs is mos'ly eejits, w'en yo wants 'em to hab some sense."

He was a huge, ill-shapen, muscular fellow, old but still vigorous, and in his small black eyes twinkled an unsounded depth of shrewdness.   He had been the colonel's slave from his young manhood to the close of the war; since then he had hung around Ellijay what time he was not sponging a livelihood from Sommerton Place under color of doing various light turns in the vegetable garden, and of attending to his quondam master's horses.

Barnaby was a great banjoist, a charming song-singer, and a leader of the negroes round about.   Lately he was gaining some reputation as a political boss.

There was but one political party in the county (for the colored people were so few that they could not be called a party), and the only struggle for office came in pursuit of a nomination, which was always equivalent to election.   Candidates were chosen at a convention or mass-meeting of the whites, and the only figure that the blacks were able to cut in the matter was by reason of a pretended rather than a real prejudice against them, which was used by the candidates (who were always white men) to further their electioneering schemes, as will presently appear.

" Hit do beat all," Barnaby repeated, shaking his heavy head reflectively, and making a grimace both comical and hideous. " Dat young man desput sma't an' cunnin', sho' 's yo' bo'n he is. He done been foolin' wid dem niggahs a'ready."

The reader may as well be told at once that if a candidate could by any means make the negroes support his opponent for the nomination it was the best card he could possibly play; or if he could not quite do this, but make it appear that the other fellow was not unpopular in colored circles, it served nearly the same turn.

Phyllis, when she ran crying upstairs after the conversation with her father, went to her room, and fell into a chair by the window. So it chanced that she overheard the conference between Colonel

Sommerton and Barnaby, and long after it was ended she still sat there leaning on the window-sill. Her eyes showed a trifle of irritation, but the tears were all gone.

" Why did n't Tom tell me that he was going to run against father?" she inquired of herself over and over. "I think he might have trusted me, so I do. It 's mean of him. And if he should beat papa! Papa could n't bear that."

She sprang to her feet and walked across the room, stopping on the way to rub her apple-bloom cheeks before a looking-glass. Vaguely enough, but insistently, the outline of a political plot glimmered in her consciousness and troubled her understanding. Plainly, her father and Tom Banister were rival candidates, and just as plainly each was scheming to make it appear that the negroes were supporting his opponent; but the girl's little head could not gather up and comprehend all that such a condition of things meant.

She supposed that a sort of disgrace would attach to defeat, and she clasped her hands and poised her winsome body melodramatically when she asked herself which she would rather the defeat would fall upon, her father or Tom. She leaned out of the window and saw Colonel Sommerton walking down the road toward town, with his cigar elevated at an acute angle with his nose, his hat pulled well down in front, by which she knew that he was still excited.

Days went by, as days will in any state of affairs, with just such faultless weather as August engenders amid the dry, cool hills of the old Cherokee country; and Phyllis noted, by an indirect attention to what she had never before been interested in, that Colonel Sommerton was growing strangely confidential and familiar with Barnaby. She had a distinct but remote impression that her father had hitherto never, at least never openly, shown such irenic solicitude in that direction, and she knew that his sudden peace-making with the old negro meant ill to her lover. She pondered the matter with such discrimination and logic as her clever little brain could compass; and at last she one evening called Barnaby to come into the garden with his banjo.

The sun was going down, and the half-grown moon swung yellow and clear against the violet arch of mid-heaven. Through the sheen a softened outline of the town wavered fantastically.

Phyllis sat on a great fragment of limestone, which, embossed with curious fossils, formed the immovable centre-piece of the garden.

Barnaby, at a respectful distance, crumpled himself satyr-like on the ground, with his banjo across his knee, and gazed expectantly aslant at the girl's sweet face.

"Now play me my father's favorite song," she said.

They heard Mrs. Wren, the house-keeper, opening the windows in the upper rooms of the mansion to let in the night air, which was stirring over the valley with a delicious mountain chill on its wings. All around in the trees and shrubbery the katydids were rasping away in immelodi-ous statement and denial of the ancient accusation.

Barnaby demurred. He did not imagine, so at least he said, that Miss Phyllis would be pleased with the ballad that recently had been the colonel's chief musical de-light; but he must obey the young lady, and so, after some throat-clearing and string-tuning, he proceeded : —

> "I 'd rudder be er niggah
>   Dan ter be er whi' man,
>   Dough the whi' man considdah
>   He se'f biggah ;
>   But ef yo' mus' be white, w'y be hones' ef yo' can,
>   An' ac' es much es poss'ble like er niggah !
>
>   "De colah ob yo' skin
>   Hit don't constertoot no sin,

> An' yo' fambly ain't er-
> Cuttin' any figgah ;
> Min' w'at yo 's er-doin', an' do de bes' yo' kin,
> An' ac' es much es poss'ble like er niggah ! "

The tune of this song was melody it-self, brimming with that unkempt, sarcas-tic humor which always strikes as if obliquely, and with a flurry of tipsy fun, into one's ears.

When the performance was ended, and the final tinkle of the rollicking banjo accompaniment died away down the slope of Sommerton Hill, Phyllis put her plump chin in her hands, and, with her elbows on her knees, looked steadily at Barnaby.

" Barn," she said, " is my father going to get the colored people to indorse Mr. Tom Banister ? "

" Yas, ma'm," replied the old negro ; and then he caught his breath and checked himself in confusion. " Da-da-dat is, er — I spec' so — er I don' 'no', ma'm," he stam-mered. " 'Fo' de Lor' I 's " —

Phyllis interrupted him with an impatient laugh, but said no more. In due time Barnaby sang her some other ditties, and then she went into the house. She gave the negro a large coin, and on the veranda steps she called back to him, " Good-night, Uncle Barn," in a voice that made him shake his head and mutter : —

" De bressed chile !   De bressed chile !"

And yet he was aware that she had outwitted him and gained his secret. He knew how matters stood between the young lady and Tom Banister, and there arose in his mind a vivid sense of the danger that might result to his own and Colonel Sommerton's plans from a disclosure of this one vital detail. Would Phyllis tell her lover ? Barnaby shook his head in a dubious way.

" Gals is pow'ful onsartin, so dey is," he muttered. " Dey tells der sweethearts mos'ly all what dey knows, spacially secrets.   Spec' de ole boss an' he plan done gone up de chimbly er-callyhootin' fo' good."

Then the old scamp began to turn over in his brain a scheme which seemed to offer him a fair way of approaching Mr. Tom Banister's pocket and the portemonnaie of Phyllis as well. He chuckled atrociously as a pretty comprehensive view of "practical politics" opened itself to him.

Tom Banister had not been to see Phyllis since her father had delivered his opinion to her touching the intrinsic merits of that young man, and she felt uneasy.

Colonel Sommerton, though notably eccentric, could be depended upon for outright dealing in general; still Phyllis had a pretty substantial belief that in politics success lay largely on the side of the trickster. For many years the colonel had been in the Legislature. No man had been able to beat him for the nomination. Phyllis had often heard him tell how he laid out his antagonists by taking excellent and popular short turns on them, and it was plain to her mind now that he was weaving a snare for Tom Banister.

She thought of Tom's running for office against her father as something prodigiously strange. Certainly it was a bold and daring piece of youthful audacity for him to be guilty of. He, a young sprig of the law, with his brown moustache not yet grown, setting himself up to beat Colonel Mobley Sommerton! Phyllis blushed whenever she thought of it; but the colonel had never once mentioned Tom's candidacy to her.

The convention was approaching, and day by day signs of popular interest in it increased as the time shortened. Colonel Sommerton was preparing a speech for the occasion. The manuscript of it lay on the desk in his library.

About this time — it was near the 1st of September, and the watermelons and cantaloupes were in their glory — the colonel was called away to a distant town for a few days. In his absence Tom Banister chanced to visit Sommerton Place. Of course Phyllis was not expecting him; indeed, she told him that he ought not to have come; but Tom thought differently in a very persuasive way. The melons were good, the library delightfully cool, and conversation caught the fragrance of innocent albeit stolen pleasure.

Tom Banister was unquestionably a handsome young fellow, carrying a hearty, whole-souled expression in his open, almost rosy face. His large brown eyes, curly brown hair, silken young moustache, and firmly set mouth and chin well matched his stalwart, symmetrical form. He was not only handsome, he was brilliant in a way, and his memory was something prodigious. Unquestionably he would rise rapidly.

" I am going to beat your father for the nomination," he remarked, midmost the discussion of their melons, speaking in a tone of absolute confidence.

"Tom," she exclaimed, "you must n't do it!"

"Why, I 'd like to know?"

She looked at him as if she felt a sudden fright. His eyes fell before her intense, searching gaze.

"It would be dreadful," she presently managed to say. "Papa could n't bear it."

"It will ruin me forever if I let him beat me. I shall have to go away from here." It was now his turn to become intense.

"I don't see what makes men think so much of office," she complained evasively. "I 've heard papa say that there was absolutely no profit in going to the Legislature." Then, becoming insistent she exclaimed, "Withdraw, Tom; please do, for my sake!"

She made a rudimentary movement as if to throw her arms around him, but it came to nothing. Her voice, however, carried a mighty appeal to Tom's heart. He looked at her, and thought how commonplace other women were when compared with her.

" You will withdraw, won't you, Tom ? " she prayed. One of her hands touched his arm. " Say yes, Tom."

For a moment his political ambition and his standing with men appeared to dissolve into a mere mist, a finely comminuted sentiment of love ; but he kept a good hold upon himself.

" I cannot do it, Phyllis," he said, in a firm voice, which disclosed by some indescribable inflection how much it pained him to refuse. " My whole future depends upon success in this race. I am sorry it is your father I must beat, but, Phyllis, I must be nominated. I can't afford to sit down in your father's shadow. As sure as you live I am going to beat him."

In her heart she was proud of him, and proud of this resolution that not even she could break.   From that moment she was between the millstones.   She loved her father, it seemed to her, more than ever, she could not bear the thought of his defeat. Indeed, with that generosity characteristic of the sex, which can be truly humorous only when absolutely unconscious of it, she wanted both Tom and the colonel nominated, and both elected.   She was the partisan on Tom's side, the adherent on her father's.

Colonel Sommerton returned on the day before the convention, and found his friends enthusiastic, all his " fences " in good condition, and his nomination evidently certain.   It followed that he was in high good-humor.   He hugged Phyllis, and casually brought up the thought of how pleasantly they could spend the winter in Atlanta when the Legislature met.

" But Tom — I mean Mr. Banister — is going to beat you, and get the nomination," she archly remarked.

"If he does, I'll deed you Sommerton Place!" As he spoke he glared at her as a lion might glare at thought of being defeated by a cub.

"To him and me?" she inquired, with sudden eagerness of tone. "If he"—

"Phyllis!" he interrupted savagely, "no joking on that subject. I won't"—

"No; I'm serious," she sweetly said. "If he can't beat you, I don't want him."

"Zounds! Is that a bargain?" He laid his hand on her shoulder, and bent down so that his eyes were on a level with hers.

"Yes," she replied; "and I'll hold you to it."

"You promise me?" he insisted.

"A man must go ahead of my papa," she said, putting her arms about the old gentleman's neck, "or I'll stay by papa."

He kissed her with atrocious violence. Even the knee-sag of his trousers suggested more than ordinary vigor of feeling.

"Well, it's good-by Tom," he said, pushing her away from him, and letting go a profound bass laugh. "I'll settle him to-morrow."

"You'll see," she rejoined. "He may not be so easy to settle."

He gave her a savage but friendly cuff as they parted.

That evening old Barnaby brought his banjo around to the veranda. Colonel Sommerton was down in town mixing with the "boys," and doing up his final political chores so that there might be no slip on the morrow. It was near eleven o'clock when he came up the hill, and stopped at the gate to hear the song that Barnaby was singing. He supposed that the old negro was all alone. Certainly the captivating voice, with its unkempt melody, and its throbbing, skipping, harum-scarum banjo accompaniment, was all that broke the silence of the place.

His song was : —

DE SASSAFRAS BLOOM.

"Dey 's sugah in de win' when de sassafras bloom,
    When de little co'n fluttah in de row,
    When de robin in de tree, like er young gal in de loom,
    Sing sweet, sing sof', sing low.

"Oh, de sassafras blossom hab de keen smell o' de root,
    An' it hab sich er tender yaller green !
    De co'n hit kinder twinkle when hit firs' begin ter shoot,
    While de bum'lebee hit bum'les in between.

"Oh, de sassafras tassel, an' de young shoot o' de co'n,
    An' de young gal er-singing in de loom,
    Dey 's somefin' 'licious in 'em f'om de day 'at dey is
        bo'n,
    An' dis darkey 's sort o' took er likin' to 'm.

"Hit 's kind o' sort o' glor'us when yo' feels so quare
        an' cur'us,
    An' yo' don' know what it is yo' wants ter do ;
    But I takes de chances on it 'at hit jes' can't be injur'us
    When de whole endurin' natur tells yo' to !

"Den wake up, niggah, see de sassafras in bloom !
    Lis'n how de sleepy wedder blow !
    An' de robin in de haw-bush an' de young gal in de
        loom
        Is er-singin' so sof' an' low."

"Thank you, Barn; here's your dollar," said the voice of Tom Banister when the song was ended. "You may go now."

And while Colonel Sommerton stood amazed, the young man came down the veranda steps with Phyllis on his arm. They stopped when they reached the ground.

"Good-night, dear. I'll win you to-morrow or my name is not Tom Banister. I'll win you, and Sommerton Place too." And when they parted he came right down the walk between the trees, to run almost against Colonel Sommerton.

"Why, good-evening, colonel," he said, with a cordial, liberal spirit in his voice. "I have been waiting in hopes of seeing you."

"You'll get enough of me to-morrow to last you a lifetime, sah," promptly responded the old man, marching straight on into the house. Nothing could express more concentrated, and yet comprehensive contempt than Colonel Sommerton's manner.

"The impudent young scamp," he growled. "I 'll show him!"

Phyllis sprang from ambush behind a vine, and covered her father's face with warm kisses, then broke away before he could say a word, and ran up to her room.

In the distant kitchen, Barnaby was singing: —

> "Kicked so high I broke my neck,
>   An' fling my right foot off'm my leg;
>   Went to work mos' awful quick,
>   An' mended 'em wid er wooden peg."

Next morning, at nine o'clock sharp, the convention was called to order, General John Tolliver in the chair. Speeches were expected, and it had been arranged that Tom Banister should first appear, Colonel Sommerton would follow, and then the ballot would be taken.

This order of business showed the fine tactics of the colonel, who well understood how much advantage lay in the vivid impression of a closing speech.

As the two candidates made their way from opposite directions through the throng to the platform, which was under a tree in a beautiful suburban grove, both were greeted with effusive warmth by admiring constituents. Many women were present, and Tom Banister felt the blood surge mightily through his veins at sight of Phyllis standing tall and beautiful before him with her hand extended.

" If you lose, die game, Tom," she murmured, as he pressed her fingers and passed on.

The young man's appearance on the stand called forth a tremendous roar of applause. Certainly he was popular. Colonel Sommerton felt a queer shock of surprise thrill along his nerves. Could it be possible that he would lose ? No ; the thought was intolerable. He sat a trifle straighter on his bench, and began gather-

ing the points of his well-conned speech.
He saw old Barnaby moving around the
rim of the crowd, apparently looking for a
seat.

Meantime Tom was proceeding in a
clear, soft, far-reaching voice. The colonel
started and looked askance. What did it
mean? At first his brain was confused,
but presently he understood. Word for
word, sentence for sentence, paragraph for
paragraph, Tom was delivering the colonel's own sonorous speech! Of course
the application was reversed here and
there, so that the wit, the humor, and the
personal thrusts all went home. It was a
wonderful piece of *ad captandum* oratory.
The crowd went wild from start to finish.

Colonel Mobley Sommerton sat dazed
and stupefied, mopping his forehead and
trying to collect his faculties. He felt
beaten, annihilated, while Tom soared su-
perbly on the wings of Sommertonian oratory so mysteriously at his command.

From a most eligible point of view Phyllis was gazing at Tom, and receiving the full brilliant current of his speech, and she appeared to catch a fine stimulus from the flow of its opening sentences. As it proceeded her face alternately flushed and paled, and her heart pounded heavily. All around rose the tumult of unbridled applause. Men flung up their hats and yelled themselves hoarse. A speech of that sort from a young fellow like Tom Banister was something to create irrepressible enthusiasm. It ended in such a din that when General John Duff Tolliver arose to introduce Colonel Sommerton he had to wait for some time to be heard.

The situation was one that absolutely appalled, though it did not quite paralyze, the old candidate, who, even after he had gained his feet and stalked to the front of the rude rostrum, was as empty of thought as he was full of despair. This sudden and unexpected appropriation of his great

speech had sapped and stupefied his intellect.   He slowly swept the crowd with his
dazed eyes, and by some accident the only
countenance clearly visible to him was that
of old Barnaby, who now sat far back on
a stump, looking for all the world like
a mightily mystified baboon.   The negro
winked and grimaced, and scratched his
flat nose in sheer vacant stupidity.   Colonel
Sommerton saw this, and it added an en-
feebling increment to his mental torpor.

" Fellow-citizens," he presently roared, in
his melodious bass voice, " I am proud of
this honor."   He was not sure of another
word as he stood with bagging trousers
and sweat-beaded face, but he made a su-
perhuman effort to call up his comatose
wits.   " I should be ungrateful were I not
proud of this great demonstration."   Just
then his gaze fell upon the face of his
daughter.   Their eyes met with a mutual
flash of retrospection.   They were remem-
bering the bargain.   The colonel was not

aware of it, but the deliberateness and vocal volume of his opening phrases made them very impressive. " I assure you," he went on, fumbling for something to say, " that my heart is brimming with gratitude, so that my lips find it hard to utter the words that crowd into my mind." At this some kindly friend in the audience gingerly set going a ripple of applause, which, though evidently forced, was like wine to the old man's intellect; it flung a glow through his imagination.

" The speech you have heard the youthful limb of the law declaim is a very good one, a very eloquent one indeed. If it were his own I should not hesitate to say right here that I ought to stand aside and let him be nominated; but, fellow-citizens, that speech belongs to another and far more distinguished and eligible man than Tom Banister." Here he paused again, and stood silent for a moment. Then, lifting his voice to a clarion pitch, he added: —

"Fellow-citizens, I wrote that speech, intending to deliver it here to-day. I was called to Canton on business early in the week, and during my absence Tom Banis-ter went to my house and got my manu-script and learned it by heart. To prove to you that what I say is true, I will now read."

At this point the colonel, after deliber-ately wiping his glasses, drew from his capacious coat-pocket the manuscript of his address, and proceeded to read it word for word, just as Banister had declaimed it. The audience listened in silence, quite unable to comprehend the situation. There was no applause. Evidently sentiment was dormant, or it was still with Tom. Colonel Sommerton, feeling the desperation of the moment, reached forth at random, and see-ing Barnaby's old black face, it amused him, and he chanced to grab a thought as if out of the expression he saw there.

"Fellow-citizens," he added, "there is

one thing I desire to say upon this impor-
tant occasion. Whatever you do, be sure
not to nominate to-day a man who would,
if elected, ally himself with the niggers.   I
don't pretend to hint that my young opponent, Tom Banister, would favor nigger
rule, but I do say — do you hear me, fellow-
citizens ? — I do say that every nigger in
this country is a Banister man!   How do
I know?   I will tell you.   Last Saturday
night the niggers had a meeting in an old
stable on my premises.   Wishing to know
what they were up to, I stole slyly to where
I could overhear their proceedings.   My
old nigger, Barnaby, — yonder he sits, and
he can't deny it, — was presiding, and the
question before the meeting was, 'Which
of the two candidates, Tom Banister and
Colonel Sommerton, shall we niggers support ? '   On this question there was some
debate and difference of opinion, until old
Bob Warmus arose and said, 'Mistah Pres'.
dent, dey's no use er-talkin'; I likes Colo-

nel Sommerton mighty well; he's a berry good man; dey's not a bit er niggah in 'im. On t' oder han', Mistah Pres'dent, Mistah Tom Banistah is er white man too, jes' de same; but I kin say fo' Mistah Banistah 'at he's mo' like er niggah 'an any white man 'at I ebber seed afore!' "

Here the colonel paused to wait for the shouting and the hat-throwing to subside. Meantime the face of old Barnaby was drawn into one indescribable pucker of amazement. He could not believe his eyes or his ears. Surely that was not Colonel Sommerton standing up there telling such an enormous falsehood on him! He shook his woolly head dolefully and gnawed a little splinter that he had plucked from a stump.

"Of course, fellow-citizens," the Colonel went on, "that settled the matter, and the niggers indorsed Tom Banister unanimously by a rising vote!"

The yell that went up when the speaker,

bowing profoundly, took his seat, made it seem certain that Banister would be beaten; but when the ballot was taken it was found that he had been chosen by one vote majority.

Colonel Mobley Sommerton's face turned as white as his hair. The iron of defeat went home to his proud heart with terrible effect, and as he tried to rise the features of the hundreds of countenances below him swam and blended confusedly on his vision. The sedentary bubbles on the knees of his trousers fluttered with sympathetic violence.

Tom Banister was on his feet in a moment. It was an appealing look from Phyllis that inspired him, and once more his genial voice rang out clear and strong.

"Fellow-citizens," he said, "I have a motion to make. Hear me." He waved his right hand to command silence, then proceeded: "Mr. President, I withdraw my name from this convention, and move that the nomination of Colonel Mobley Sommerton be made unanimous by acclamation. I have no right to this nomination, and nothing, save a matter greater than life or death to me, could have induced me to steal it as I this day have done. Colonel Sommerton knows why I did it. He gave his word of honor that he would cease all objections to giving his daughter to me in marriage, and that furthermore he would deed Sommerton Place to us as a wedding-present, if I beat him for the nomination. Mr. President and fellow-citizens, do you blame me for memorizing his speech? That magnificent speech meant to me the most beautiful wife in America, and the handsomest estate in this noble county."

If Tom Banister had been boisterously applauded before this, it was as nothing beside the noise which followed when Colonel Sommerton was declared the unanimous nominee of the convention. Meantime Phyllis had hurried to the carriage and been driven home: she dared not stay and let the crowd gaze at her after that bold confession of Tom's.

The cheering for the nominee was yet at its flood when Banister leaped at Colonel Sommerton and grasped his hand. The old gentleman was flushed and smiling, as became a politician so wonderfully favored. It was a moment never to be forgotten by either of the men.

"I cordially congratulate you, Colonel Sommerton, on your nomination," said Tom, with great feeling, "and you may count on my hearty support."

"If I don't have to support you, and pay your office rent in the bargain, all the rest of my life, I miss my guess, you young scamp!" growled the colonel, in a major key. "Be off with you!"

Tom moved away to let the colonel's friends crowd up and shake hands with him; but the delighted youth could not withhold a Parthian shaft. As he retreated he said : "Oh, Colonel Sommerton, don't bother about my support; Sommerton Plantation will be ample for that!"

"Hit do beat all thunder how dese white men syfoogles eroun' in politics," old Barnaby thought to himself. Then he rattled the coins in his two pockets. The contributions of Colonel Sommerton chinked on the left, those of Tom Banister and Phyllis rang on the right.

"Blame this here ole chile's eyes," he went on, "but 't war a close shabe! Seem lak I 's kinder holdin' de balernce ob power. I use my infloonce fer bofe ob 'em — yah, yah, yah-r-r! an' hit did look lak I 's gwin ter balernce fings up tell I 'lec' 'em bofe ter oncet right dar! Bofe ob 'em got de nomernation — yah, yah, yah-r-r! But I say 'rah fo' little Miss Phyllis! She de one 'at know how to pull de right string — yah, yah, yah-r-r!"

The wedding at Sommerton Place came on the Wednesday following the fall election.   Besides the great number of guests and the striking beauty of the bride, there was nothing notable in it, unless the song prepared by Barnaby for the occasion, and sung by him thereupon to a captivating banjo accompaniment, may be so distinguished.   A stanza, the final one of that masterpiece, has been preserved.   It may serve as an informal ending, a charcoal tailpiece, to our light but truthful little story.

" Stan' by yo' frien's and nebber mek trouble,
    An' so, ef yo 's got any sense,
  Yo 'll know hit 's a good t'ing ter be sorter double,
    An' walk on bofe sides ob de fence ! "